Gillian Leaving

Lucy Nankivell

© Lucy Nankivell 2016

Lucy Nankivell has asserted her moral right to be identified as the author of this book in accordance with Section 77 of the Copyright, Designs and Patents Act 1988.

All rights reserved. No part of this book may be reproduced in any manner without written permission except in the case of brief quotations included in critical articles and reviews. For information, please contact the author.

All characters appearing in this work are fictitious. Any resemblance to real persons, living or dead, is purely coincidental.

For Peter

Acknowledgments

I would like to thank my good friends and fellow copy-editors Clare Weze, Judith Shaw, Alison Hardy and Claire Jordan for their helpful suggestions on this book; and Clare Weze in particular for her meticulous proofreading.

Thanks to my husband, Peter, for designing the front cover and giving so much help and support throughout.

Contents

Acknowledgments	4
Contents	5
1: Waking	6
2: Moving	15
3: Calais	21
4: The Dunes	26
5: The Tide	31
6: The River	42
7: The Town of Blue	57
8: History	66
9: Omelette and Apple Pie	75
10: Work	93
11: Summer	98
12: Hervé	113
13: Rain	132
14: Emily	136
15: Words	145
16: The Dark House	153
17: Ghislaine	162

1: Waking

Get out. Get out now.

She heard the words so clearly, surely someone must have spoken them. But there was nobody: only herself and the walls, and the familiar fear lying over her like a dank blanket.

And yet something had changed. She sat up and found the light switch straight away, no groping across the blackness expecting something to come slithering up from under the bed and grab her arm. She saw it was just after three, and didn't quail at the thought of the sleepless hours ahead and the alarm going off at seven. She reached for the glass of water that she ritually placed by her bed every night, took a long drink and lay back, thinking.

At half past eight the office of JF Evans Accounting was open and people were starting to arrive; some morose, some loudly cheerful, most in that state of grim endurance that February mornings bring. Nobody noticed anything unusual about Gillian Bailie, who always crept in looking as if she hoped not to be seen at all, and was always silently at work while others were still hanging up their coats and exchanging ritual jokes. As usual, she remained crouched over her desk until eleven precisely and then stood up. The only difference was that instead of going to the coffee machine, she slipped an envelope out of her bag and went, clutching it, to tap on the manager's door.

Daniel glanced up as she entered in answer to his shout of 'Come in!' As always he found the sight of Gillian's meek face vaguely irritating, but today she didn't poke her head sheepishly round the door and then, on being invited, gradually let the rest of her follow. She walked straight in, handed him the envelope she was holding and, murmuring something about 'if you wouldn't mind' was gone almost before he had read his name on the front.

Inside was a very brief, very formal letter stating that she wished to give a month's notice for personal reasons. Not a man who took much interest in the private lives of his staff, Daniel was startled into speculation. She certainly didn't look pregnant, and why would she simply be giving in her notice without a word if that were the reason? Terminal illness? lottery win? – though if the latter, she would surely be looking a bit more cheerful, not to mention having bought herself some new clothes or something. Anyway, it was all in order so there was nothing to do but accept it.

He caught up with her later that morning, peering into the depths of the photocopier.

'I'm sorry you're leaving us, Gillian.' It was true up to a point – she was conscientious, inoffensive and, despite her appearance, rarely ill, besides being less inefficient than she seemed – but a matter for mild annoyance rather than sorrow. Still. He searched for something more concrete to say and came up with: 'And we'll certainly miss you looking after the website.'

She looked up with a nervous smile and then back at the copier, hovering a finger over the button for several seconds and then dabbing at it; she performed even routine tasks as if she were trying them for the first time and expecting to fail. 'I hope,' Daniel asked in his best communication-seminar manner, 'that there isn't anything, er, wrong?'

'Oh no,' said Gillian at once, 'thank you, Daniel, there's nothing wrong at all. It's just ... something I have to do. By the way, would you mind not mentioning it to anyone for a few days?'

'Of course, of course,' said Daniel, hastily backing away in case she might be about to unburden her soul over the copy paper.

It was already dark when Gillian, a little behind the others as usual, saved her work, shut down and headed for the car park. She drove as anxiously as she did everything else, but the ten-mile journey from Evans' was one of the few that she knew well enough to take calmly. Until she was clear of the suburbs there was still the rush-hour traffic to negotiate, but before long she was moving between fields, sharing the narrow lanes of her childhood with only a few commuters, and her mind was free to wrestle with a new worry: whatever was she going to tell Aunt Emily? She passed along the wider avenue through the big housing estate and into old Southash, the *real* village that contained everyone and everything that mattered to Emily, still with no idea what she was going to say.

She couldn't remember ever approaching the house without a jolt of anxiety; this square mid-Victorian building, big enough for a large family, yet where she still managed, hourly, to get on her aunt's nerves. But tonight was far worse; her stomach tightened and her hands grew clammy on the wheel as she inched up the drive.

In the end when she let herself in and heard the familiar greeting of 'You're late!' she lost her nerve. She muttered something about changing, went straight to her room and sat on the bed for a long while without moving. The thought of what she had done paralysed her – she who was liable to have a sleepless night if she didn't return a colleague's greeting warmly enough or forgot to read all her emails. But she had done it; and now there was time to think about the consequences.

The more she thought, the less sense it made. Why had she woken up in the night, heard a voice telling her to get out, and then got up in the morning and blithely left the firm where she had worked for most of her adult life? That she might go on a journey, any journey, by herself – just pack a case, get a ticket and set off – was an idea as audacious and terrifying as she could imagine. She got up, went to the window and closed the curtains on the back garden. This garden, this house, this room with its solid, outdated furniture, unchanged since before she was born: how many nights had she even spent away from here? She turned slowly back towards the bed, picked up her bag and felt inside it for her phone. She couldn't hide in here forever; if she didn't have the nerve to tell Aunt Emily yet, at least she could tell Kate.

'You're going to France? That's lovely, Gill, it's about time you had a holiday. Where exactly are you going then?'

Where indeed? And yet she heard herself answering breezily, 'Well, I thought I'd go by car and just drive around for a few weeks – explore a bit.'

There was a brief silence. Then Kate's voice, a little cooler than before, said, 'It's not like you to try and wind me up, Gill, and I really don't have time for—'

Gillian couldn't bear to annoy Kate, who tended to treat her like one of her own children even though they were almost the same age. She rushed to appease her: 'No, no, Kate, I'm not joking. In fact I' – this part was going to be difficult – 'I, er, gave in my notice today.'

'You did *what*?'

'Gave in my notice. Yes.'

'For god's sake, Gill, what is it? Are you ill?'

'No, no, I've never been better, it's …' As usual, she waited for her friend to tell her what to do; to explain the world to her.

Kate didn't let her down. 'Why don't you come over and tell me about it? Come tonight if you like – Al's out, and the anklebiters'll be off to bed soon.'

'You know I'd love to see Martha and Jack – thanks so much, I'll come after dinner – about eight? And I'll try and be making more sense by then.'

She went back to the living room. Now it was time to tell her. Aunt Emily, I've just given in my notice and I'm going to drive to France as soon as I can get a passport. What's for dinner?

Aunt Emily glanced up from the knitting that always made her look less like a cosy old lady than a tricoteuse crouching beneath the guillotine. 'I've left you a plate in the oven,' she said, 'since you're so late.' Gillian said, 'Oh, thank you, Aunt Emily, I'm sorry about being late – we were so busy today. I'm just popping over to Kate's afterwards for a bit, I ... I think she wants some help with her laptop or something.' This was both craven and unfair, since Kate never needed help with anything.

Emily sniffed. She detested Kate, a bumptious incomer who called her elders and betters by their first names without permission, and pronounced Southash South-Ash instead of rhyming it with brothersh as the real villagers did.

Kate and Al lived in one of the family houses on the estate which, though it had been there as long as Gillian could remember and was officially part of the village, still outraged Aunt Emily and her peers. Their two small children came rushing to the door demanding, in random order, sweets, stories and games – nervous and awkward with children, she found it easiest to give them whatever they asked for, as Jack and Martha were well aware. She sat on the floor with them while they competed for her attention, and when they were hauled off to bed by their mother, who believed in strict routines, tidied up the mess of toys and plastic mugs.

'So,' said Kate when the house was quiet and the two of them were sitting in the living room with coffee.

'So.' Gillian paused a moment, then began uncertainly, 'I'm going to spend a month or two travelling around France – maybe somewhere else too, it depends – and then, well, I'll see what happens.'

'All right, but for a start why do you need to leave your job?'

'Because—' She wanted to say the words that had been in her head ever since they woke her in the night: *I've got to get out*. But in the face of Kate's brisk capability they were just too silly to say aloud.

'Oh, because it's about time I did something new, isn't it? Haven't you told me so often enough?'

Kate was looking at her in astonishment. 'Well, yes,' she said, 'I know I'm always nagging you about living a bit, but I was thinking you might take up dancing, try speed-dating – I don't know, I never expected you to drop everything and take off on your own! It wasn't me lecturing you that put this into your head, was it?'

'No, no, it's me. I'm not worried about leaving Evans': I won't miss the place and I'm qualified, I'll get another job. I've saved plenty, I could go six or eight months without any trouble. I might even find something in France.'

'That's the other thing – why does it have to be France? I mean, you haven't even been abroad in your life: you must be about the only person left under ninety who hasn't—'

'Well, there you are! You did once say I lived like an old lady, didn't you? It's because I've always spent my holidays with Aunt Emily, and now – well, that's just it, I never felt like travelling on my own, and there wasn't anyone I could go with. But I always wanted to go to France more than anywhere.' It felt strange to be talking about her life, talking so much about anything – had she ever done it before? 'Maybe it's because of my mother. She taught French in Southampton, did you know?'

'No, you've never talked about your parents at all that I know of.'

Well, of course I don't remember them. But she did teach French and …'

'And what?'

Gillian realised she had drifted into silence. 'Oh, nothing. Anyway, later I wanted to do a French degree too.'

'I thought you did business and admin at the college. Did you change because Emily thought that would be more use to you?'

'She did, but that was only part of it. I did apply to study French and then when they started talking about the year abroad, when I really thought about having to go and live in France for a year' – she looked down, blushing, and took a gulp of coffee – 'it's so stupid but I just lost my nerve. I'd probably have been working in a school, and ... well.'

'Remembering the way we treated those poor French assistants at my school, you were probably right – can't see you standing up to a classful of teenagers,' said Kate, looking pityingly at her. 'All the same, I'm surprised you never mentioned it.'

'I just felt such a fool,' she said lightly. 'But anyway, I've always loved reading about France and I used to read in French, all the novels and things we did on the course. So now I thought I'd go and see some of the places I'd read about.'

'You're amazing, you know,' said Kate. 'In this day and age ... you remind me of, of a young lady in a costume drama or something. You do know it's 2007, don't you? People are going on day trips to Paris and weekends to New York, and here you are contemplating this great adventure of travelling eleven miles across the Channel. Come to think of it, you're the one who knows all that Victorian stuff, but isn't there a book that starts like that? Not Jane Eyre, but something like it?'

Gillian looked up with a sudden smile. 'Yes, *Villette*. Only that's to Belgium, but you're right, it is a bit like me. Well, maybe I'll fall in love with a short French professor as well.'

'Is that what happens? Well, it's more likely than meeting anyone living here.' Another pitying look; 'meeting someone before it's too late' was something Kate urged on Gillian almost as often as 'finding a new interest', 'doing something about your look/hair/posture' and 'taking an assertiveness course'.

'I bet Emily got a shock when you told her.'

'The thing is I haven't told her yet. She'll get so upset, I thought if I could tell her when it was all fixed ...'

'Or do you mean you'd tell her when it was too late to scare you out of it?' Another of Kate's frequent pieces of advice was to stop letting herself be bullied by her aunt.

Gillian smiled faintly. 'I suppose I am just putting it off. But I'll tell her tonight. Besides, we'll need to find someone to come and help her in the house while I'm gone.'

Emily was still up when she came in. 'Well,' she said, 'have you put Kate's computer together again? You should have, the time you've taken.'

Gillian forced herself to come in and sit down instead of fleeing to her room again, drew a breath and said, 'Aunt Emily, there's something I'd like to tell you.' Emily looked up but carried on knitting. Stammering and feeling herself going red, Gillian explained her plans. Her aunt listened without interruption, but her nose seemed to grow sharper as Gillian blundered on.

There was silence for a while except for the clack of needles. Then Emily said, 'I suppose I should have expected you'd do something silly like this. After all, it's just the sort of thing your mother would have done.'

'Aunt Emily ...'

'Not now, Gillian, not now.' She pushed her needles into the mass of grey wool and got up. 'I'm tired and I'm going to bed. We can discuss this in the morning.'

Awake and restless that night, Gillian thought about freedom. Here she was, single, childless, healthy, fairly well educated and not poor. Who should feel free if not she? And yet she barely understood the meaning of the word. Lying in the dark, it was as if she saw the bars of a cage around her bed; as if they had always been there, but she was only aware of them now because, at long last, she was trying to move.

Which meant that everything she did from now on, every step beyond the cage door, would be a new adventure.

2: Moving

'You'll need special lights for France,' said Al, 'deflectors. Or something. And have you ever driven on the right?'

Gillian, who had scarcely driven anywhere except to the office and back for the last three years, and nowhere at all before that, smiled weakly and turned to a more hopeful subject. 'My passport's all right anyway,' she said, 'I paid for the express service and it's just come back. And at this time of year it looks like I can book the tunnel or the ferry more or less at the last minute, so as soon as I decide when I want to go—'

'So what's the plan now? Kate tells me you haven't got anywhere you want to see especially.' Al was always very kind and tactful towards her; if Kate tended to treat her like a child, Al seemed rather to think of her as a slightly dotty old lady. She suspected that he was trying hard not to let her know that he thought her temporarily insane, or that, guided by his wife, he still didn't believe she would actually go to France at all in the end. She could almost hear Kate telling him: 'Humour her, Al, it's a sort of biological clock thing – she's just realised life's been passing her by, so now she's desperate to do something before it's too late. But drive to France on her own? This is Gill we're talking about, she won't even reverse out of our drive on her own! Just play along, and she'll drop the idea soon and go for a nice Club Med trip instead.'

'Well, I thought I'd just start from the north and see what happens. I'm going to take the Tunnel and start from Calais – I thought I might spend a few days on the Opal Coast, maybe do some walking. Then just go down the west coast – Brittany, the Vendée – see how far I get.' She had a vision of herself wandering through the sand dunes, hair blown in the breeze, looking down at the bright sea, and for the first time thought: this is real, I can do it.

Kate came in with a dish of spaghetti carbonara. 'Have you got your travel insurance yet then?'

Abruptly Gillian came down from the dunes – it was exactly these details, these *grown-up* things like insurance and mortgages and papers, which so terrified her that she was still living in her childhood home and rarely took a longer journey than to the nearest Sainsbury's and back. And now she was going to deal with these things all alone ...

Al rescued her. 'You just need an E111 from the post office, Gillian, and if you want anything else just Google "France Travel Insurance". Same with everything really. If I were you I'd be more worried about whether the car's all right.'

'Now that is a point.' Kate paused in dishing out the pasta. 'Do you think that old Micra's up to it? I know Emily never went further than the end of the village in it, but it's pretty ancient.'

'Well, I think it will be all right for what I'm doing. That's the thing, I'm going to take it all very slowly. I don't even need to go on the – what's it called? autoroute; everyone says the French roads are so good, and anyway what does it matter? I can spend half the day going twenty miles if I want to. I don't expect to go long distances – if I did I'd probably take the train. Besides,' she added with an attempt at airiness, 'I'll have to get used to driving on the right.'

'You're not exactly used to driving on the left, be honest!' said Kate rather sharply.

Gillian looked at her, a little hurt. 'I know that, Kate, but I'm still going to do it,' she said.

Kate shrugged. 'Sorry – hey, maybe I'm jealous. When did we last go off on an adventure, Al?'

'Did we ever?' Al said and then laughed. After a moment, Kate joined in. 'Anyway,' she said, 'to your adventure, Gill!' and picked up her wineglass. They all drank, awkwardly, and there was a little silence. 'So,' Al asked Gillian, 'when do you leave?'

'In about three weeks, I hope – I'm leaving work in a fortnight and then I want another week to get ready. It'll be April then, I thought that would be a nice time to go.' She didn't tell them that she was secretly taking special driving lessons to try and get her confidence up, nor that in the last session her instructor had snapped that she wasn't to be trusted in Tesco car park, let alone on the autoroute.

When she got up to go, Kate said, 'The main thing is to take your laptop so you can send us messages. And pictures of you cavorting on the Riviera. And' – she hesitated and then hurried on – 'I *don't* want to put you off, but if anything goes wrong just give us a call. We're always here, you know.'

'I know. And thank you, thank you both.'

During her last weeks at work Daniel was still behaving with embarrassed sympathy and visibly longing for her to be gone – probably, she suspected, in case she dropped dead on the spot or went into some sort of fit. Being an object of speculation was a new sensation to her – from some odd looks she got, she was fairly sure that he had passed on his suspicions – and she was surprised to find that she didn't dislike it. Whoever looked at her at all, least of all as a thing of mystery? In the quieter moments she even toyed with the idea of dropping a few tantalising hints.

The final few days were rather subdued. Now that she was committed – her ticket booked, her hotel reservation made for the first two nights and, as far as she knew, all her papers in order – there seemed no point in not letting everyone know why she was leaving. But when she did tell colleagues about her planned French adventure, it didn't seem to strike them as very noteworthy; their reactions didn't go beyond 'Oh? That sounds nice.' Whatever they had imagined as her reason for leaving, it had obviously been more exciting than that. Of course, other people went off on these trips all the time and thought nothing of it. Now, saying quiet goodbyes to the few people who might have been called her friends – those whose names she knew, at least – it was brought home to her how little impression she had ever made at JF Evans Accounting. She remembered the times when others had left and there had been a little ceremony – the leaver had brought in a bottle of wine, or there had been a visit to the pub after work or even a whip-round for a present. It wasn't that she was disliked, she knew that perfectly well; it was only that she was transparent, insignificant. It had been this way all her life; she should be used to it. Sometimes she heard women in their forties lamenting that they were starting to feel invisible and was always puzzled: what was it like to feel anything else?

Well, she thought as she cleared her desk and started to look in her bag for her car keys, it would be to her advantage from now on. She would go wherever she liked, and if no one ever noticed her she would be able to watch and listen and enjoy all the drama of life undisturbed.

Only, wouldn't it also be nice to take part in it? Well, never mind. She picked up her few belongings, took a last look at the rows of workstations and walked out of JF Evans, unnoticed.

All she had to do now was try one more time to reconcile her aunt to the trip. Aunt Emily hadn't moved an inch from her first reaction of icy disapproval, though over the last weeks she'd managed to come up with a good many new reasons for it. Without actually saying so, she made it clear that she thought her niece was going to France in search of wild sexual adventures. This hadn't occurred to Gillian before, but she agreed with her aunt that anything could happen. Then Emily had listed every possible thing that could go wrong, from car crashes to deadly diseases, and Gillian continued to agree until Emily gave up, exhausted. She had discovered long ago that this was so much easier than trying to argue with an elderly woman who had an unlimited fund of criticism and very little to do with her time. 'All I'll say,' she had ended inaccurately, 'is that you'll only have yourself to blame if it all ends in tears.'

Now, driving back to Southash, as always Gillian found herself rehearsing polite phrases. At least this time there would be no need to search for anecdotes or find questions to keep the conversation going, since Emily at least would surely have plenty to say.

She gave a rerun of all her previous objections to the plan, with one addition. 'Well,' she concluded with a sigh, 'if you insist on going I can't stop you. And there's no need to worry about me. I'll be quite all right.'

Gillian was appalled at her own heartlessness. In fact it had never really occurred to her that Aunt Emily wouldn't be all right. She always seemed perfectly healthy, and as absorbed as ever in her house, in the task of keeping up appearances, and in the complicated network of wary friendships, feuds and alliances that had made up her whole life since long before Gillian was born. She rarely gave any sign of enjoying her niece's presence in the house, still less of depending on her: Gillian had plenty of regular tasks and errands, certainly, but they were carried out under instructions. There was never any question of who was in charge. But now she looked across at her aunt and for the first time saw, not the face of authority but a lonely woman nearing eighty; and yes, when you really looked at her she did seem frail. And if she was lonely she would never say so.

'Auntie,' said Gillian, for once using the forbidden term, 'you know Jenny's ready to come in every other day, or as often as you want – I've left her number on the hall table – but *will* you be all right on your own?'

Old and frail or not, Emily disliked sympathy as much as ever. 'Of course I will,' she snapped, ignoring the first part of the sentence, 'when am I ever ill? And how much help have I ever asked from you? It's yourself you should be worrying about – a woman your age with no husband, no job, no friends except for that ghastly girl from the estate. And now you're proposing to waste all your savings on this silly trip, you won't have a penny to your name soon. Are you expecting *me* to keep you?'

The moment of weakness was clearly past.

As she started her packing Gillian was distracted by questions that had never occurred to her before. She had always accepted their relationship without much thought – what else had she ever known? But now she found herself wondering: what, deep down, did Emily think about her? Was there affection under the coldness? Was the constant criticism a form of concern? As a young child she had wanted to feel that she was loved and welcome in her home, like the children at school, but she had never quite managed to believe it. She was different; she knew it and so did they. Other children burst into the house at the end of the school day, shrieking out news, demands, plans. She crept in, wiping her feet repeatedly, putting away her satchel before she could be rebuked. Other children played together on the patch of field in front of the school, or met up in the lanes after dinner on summer evenings and headed for the wood. She walked to and from school in silence, head down as if the taunts that fell on her were stinging rain.

When she grew up the taunts had stopped, but nothing else had really changed. Well, if she was to walk in silence all her life, at least she could choose to walk somewhere different for a while.

3: Calais

It wasn't light yet. Gillian drove jerkily on towards Folkestone, forcing herself not to clench the wheel and trying to tame the growing panic by analysing it. What was it about motorways that so terrified her? The speed, she supposed; somehow she had never got used to the idea of objects moving at so much more than human pace. The need for instant decisions, exhausting to one who dithered over every choice. And then there was the aggression that followed her everywhere; behind every wheel lurked a dark impatience that would turn to malevolence if the driver in front hesitated for a split second. She had thought herself so clever, booking a 6 a.m. crossing when the roads would be nice and empty, except that they weren't, the motorway was alive with roaring psychopaths in armoured vehicles and they were all chasing after her tiny, eggshell-fragile green Micra...

A lorry pulled out ahead of her and she settled in behind it – she seemed to recall being told that following lorries wasn't really all that safe, but they always made her feel obscurely protected. Also, as this one appeared to be German, there was a fair chance it was headed for the Tunnel too, and she could amble along in its slipstream all the way. She loosened her grip on the wheel again – if it was a rabbit it would have been long dead, she remembered the driving instructor telling her – took several deep, soothing breaths and reminded herself for the tenth time of Al's last warning: not the *Dartford* Tunnel.

And then suddenly there were signs everywhere, signs nobody could mistake: reassuring blue pictures of cars, lorries and caravans, and CHANNEL TUNNEL in large helpful letters. She let out a long sigh and drove on; it was almost five now. She passed more signs: TERMINAL 20 MILES ... TERMINAL 15 MILES ... in a few minutes she would be in the terminal and then she could relax before the ordeal of the tunnel itself.

The terminal, the whole complex, was huge – at first sight it looked like an immense sports area, laid out with white lines for some incomprehensible form of tennis. Gillian slowed to a halt, was blasted by a furious horn behind her, slapped her foot down and lurched forward. In her haste she joined the first queue she saw, realised she was now surrounded by caravans and had to shoot out again, forcing an enraged caravanner to try and swerve. By now her hands were sweating so she could hardly grip the wheel at all, and for a moment it occurred to her just to turn round and follow the signs back out again. They couldn't *make* you go, could they?

But then there was another queue which seemed to be full of cars, so she joined that. Now there was a long wait – plenty of time to start a fresh panic, over documents this time. Fumbling in the envelope where all her precious papers were kept, she dropped the lot on the floor, scrabbling under the seat to retrieve her passport just as the queue moved forward again; so she left it all there, drove forward another three feet and started the wait all over again. When she did reach the ticket window she parked too far away from it and had to manoeuvre shakily back again, almost backing into the car behind, then handed the official a wad of documents in a hopeful 'take a card, any card' spirit which he didn't seem to appreciate. However, he accepted her ticket, handed her a mysterious piece of paper with a letter J on it, said 'Departure in forty minutes' and waved her away.

She followed the signs to the car park, where there was enough space even for her to pull up without mishap and, copying the other cars, hung her J from the rear view mirror. Then, clutching fistfuls of papers and euros, she headed for the terminal building itself. She hadn't dared to ask the peeved official what the letter was for, but no doubt the answer was to be found in here.

There seemed to be message boards everywhere. After a while she worked out that the giant letters were there to tell you when to rejoin the queue, and that as a J she probably had time for a coffee; but she was still too nervous to do anything in case she suddenly turned round and found that J had disappeared from the boards and They wouldn't let her on the train any more. So she crept around the vast building, looking at the rows of bottles and stacks of chocolates in the duty-free shops. It suddenly struck her that she was very hungry, having been up since three o'clock on nothing but a mug of tea, but again she didn't dare risk getting one of the hot croissants or sticky buns that were piled up on the counters of the coffee shops.

Mounting panic made her feel hot and stifled; all at once she was fighting for breath. She staggered outside to take in great gulps of the cold air and stayed there in a daze, looking out over the huge car park and trying to grasp what she was doing here; and came back in to find that she had managed to miss the summons after all.

A race to the car and a short, jerky drive later, she found herself in a motionless queue once more, and wondered if she need have worried. Finally, with only one tense moment when the customs officer looked suspiciously at her passport, she was allowed to inch onto the train and up to the car in front; although, slightly losing control of the brake, she did nearly crush the fragile-looking uniformed woman who was beckoning her forward and seemingly urging her to push up against the next bumper.

She had expected to be even more terrified in the tunnel, constantly imagining the roar of black water overhead – indeed she had half expected that passengers would be peering out into it as if through some kind of porthole. But it was so difficult to believe you were under the sea, Gillian soon forgot that she was, and began to relax slightly for the first time since being shrieked awake by that three o'clock alarm. Now it was after six ... seven! French time – she hurriedly adjusted her watch, looked at her passport again (would they want to see it on the other side?) and spread the Europe atlas out on the passenger seat. Not that it would do her much good at first, as driving on the right was going to take all her attention. She would just have to let the road take her along and worry about finding the hotel later.

And now, incredibly, they were slowing down. Of course she'd been told the crossing only took thirty-five minutes, but her mind still wouldn't grasp it. Just over half an hour to make the journey that in her mind had always been an impassable barrier. On one side lay the south of England, the shires, her own narrow path between the prison of her aunt's house and the even smaller cage of her working day; shopping for sensible meals and sensible clothes, going to the library and walking alone in the park at safe times. On the other side was a world she had imagined while going quietly through her prescribed days – a world where the colours were brighter, people lived their lives more intensely and took time over their pleasures. She had no idea whether what she would find on the other side of the sea would be anything like the pictures she had made for herself, but did that matter? As the overhead notice boards changed to 'Bon Voyage' and she prepared to start the car again, she thought of the words of Candide, the eternal optimist: 'If we find nothing pleasant, at least we shall find something new.'

When the cars emerged from the tunnel, it was full daylight. Gillian just drove, with no clear idea of what to do next. It was surprisingly easy – signs directed her away from CALAIS-CENTRE and towards BOULOGNE, and with a stream of traffic to follow there was no trouble about keeping to the right. And along with the terror she felt a surge of excitement. I'm here, this is France, that's Calais, I'm in France. The words made a jingle in her head: I'm here, this is France.

4: The Dunes

As soon as she saw the knife-and-fork image on a road sign, Gillian pulled over. Everything seemed so much larger than in England – the road so wide and almost empty, even though it was past eight now, the service station, even the parking spaces; there was just more of everything. More space, more light.

The tank was still a third full, but rather than take any chances she went to fill it up before doing anything else. Getting petrol was one of those everyday tasks that she found inexplicably hard; something always seemed to go wrong, like the hose not stretching or the fuel door getting stuck. Now there was a new source of alarm: she had always thought the French word for petrol was *l'essence*, and to be offered a choice between *carburant* and *gazole* was baffling. Surely *gazole* was petrol? She hovered between the two for a painful moment before she remembered from her guidebook that it was diesel.

Once the car was fed, she managed to spot the kiosk, pay for the fuel and find a parking space without mishap. Then, feeling less nervous as well as extremely hungry, she went to the counter in the restaurant section to make her very first order in French. Asking for a *petit dejeuner complet* presented no difficulties, but she couldn't understand a word of the reply. '*Pardon?*' Gillian pleaded, feeling exactly as she had when called on to answer questions at school. Visibly irritated, the woman snapped 'Orange juice?' in perfect English. Gillian meekly accepted, and handed over a fifty-euro note to avoid having to try to understand the price. The assistant looked at it coldly and said, 'Do you have something smaller?' Gillian fumbled in her wallet and three more notes fluttered out onto the counter. The assistant picked up the smallest with an air of disgust, smacked it into the till and spilled the change onto Gillian's tray. She whimpered

'Merci' and fled to a table near the window, feeling quite disproportionately upset – how was she ever to manage if she couldn't even understand the simplest question? and was everyone going to get annoyed with her so quickly? The croissant, orange juice and coffee on her tray looked dismally inadequate too, and the surroundings could have been any transport café, anywhere at all. Her mood of elation was quite gone.

She took a sip of the coffee, nibbled a corner of the slightly stale croissant and felt stronger. She looked around at the light filling the room – yellower, surely, than the light she was used to? – and told herself: I am in a new country, seeing new places and new people. I am starting a new life.

She tried to hold on to that as she left the building. After wandering around for some minutes deciphering the signs, she managed to work out the way to the exit for Hardelot, and once back in the car and studying the map, was relieved to find that she wouldn't need to take the autoroute. She really wasn't up to using toll roads yet. Never mind, she was starting a new life.

The panic hit without warning as she put the key in the ignition. It was like a physical presence threatening to push her right out of the car; she braced herself against the seat and fought for breath. Sit still, sit back, that's it ... deep breath, take a rest, close your eyes. The moment they closed she saw lines, mad jumbled arrows and letters all hurtling towards her, coming alive in a frenzy of furious hoots and yells and waving fists. I can't do this, I can't I can't ...

This is ridiculous, said Aunt Emily's voice. *What on earth are you afraid of? People do this every day.*

I'm not like other people.

Stop dramatising yourself! There's nothing wrong with you except laziness and cowardice.

I tell you I can't.

After a while she opened her eyes and straightened herself. Here she was: her choices were to go on or stay here until ... until, presumably, someone came and carted her away, and probably had her locked up as well.

'And what seems to be the trouble with this patient?'

'Apparently she doesn't like driving, doctor.'

Gillian began to giggle as she shakily turned the key and fastened her seatbelt.

It was past eleven before she reached Hardelot, after several wrong turnings and two pauses for sitting in an aire, breathing deeply to subdue the terror that kept coming back. Once off the Route Nationale she found herself in deep countryside, thankfully almost empty so there was time to slow right down and read the road signs. Condette, Hardelot, then Rue de la Plage, and suddenly there it was, Hotel Plage. Her first French destination – almost her first independent destination ever, come to think of it – reached with scarcely a hitch.

Check-in was easy, if disappointing, since the receptionist spoke fluent English and had no intention of giving her guest any free French practice. Before long Gillian was established in a quiet, unremarkable but comfortable room; she stretched out on the bed to test it, closed her eyes and opened them, surely only moments later, with no idea where she was.

In that confused moment she felt the full reality of what she was doing; lying in the half-dark with the curtains drawn, hundreds of miles from home for the first time in her life. She groped for her watch, saw with incredulity that she had slept for over three hours and lay back, trying to assimilate the thought: Nobody knows where I am. I'm not going to see anyone I know, there is nothing I have to do, nowhere I have to be, all day long.

She pushed aside the fact that she also had no job, no home and no friends within hundreds of miles. It would still be hours till dinner; it was time to go and make that picture come true, the one that had stayed with her all across the Channel: herself standing in the windblown sand dunes, looking down at the sea. All at once she had a purpose, a task; filled with what she would not let herself call relief, she jumped up, went to the window and tugged back the curtains. The only view was of the opposite wall; never mind. She found her thick walking shoes and, as if she had an appointment in the dunes and dared not be late, hurried down the stairs and out into the sharp, windy afternoon.

Intent on her new mission, she paid the town little attention for the moment; LA PLAGE was clearly marked and she followed the signs unthinkingly. It was only a few minutes' walk to the promenade, and only a short way along that the dunes began. Walking among the young families and cyclists on the promenade, she was aware again of the larger scale of everything compared to southern England; the sky seemed higher, the sea to stretch further, and with so much space there was no bad-tempered jostling between the riders and walkers.

In the dunes there were far fewer people, only the occasional dog owner. It felt colder out here. Gillian sat down in a sheltered hollow and looked around; it was much greener than she had imagined, a billow of grass and sand rising as high as she could see behind her. The sand was clammy to the touch. In front of her the sea wasn't shimmering blue as in the dream, but choppy and grey; the wind was raw and she felt – the word was in her mind before she could banish it – miserable. 'You're supposed to be starting a new life,' she reminded herself sternly, and then realised that she had spoken aloud and a pair of walkers were just passing her on the narrow path. They responded with *'Bonjour, Madame'* and passed on.

She *was* miserable, what was the use of pretending? She'd come on a ridiculous whim to a country which she knew next to nothing about – where had she got her ideas of France except through old novels and Truffaut films and silly stilted school textbooks? And on the first day she was already tired of being alone, unable to find things to do to pass the time, just like – she could almost hear Aunt Emily saying it – a spoilt child whining for someone to come and amuse her. The hugeness of the landscape, so exciting on the drive here, felt unsettling now; she felt watched, judged and found inadequate. Whatever was she going to do here for weeks, for months, when even one day was intolerably long?

'What you need,' she said, aloud again, since there was nobody on the path now, 'is a cup of tea.' Surely in this town full of British visitors – even in April she had passed several already in the hotel and the streets – it would be possible to find such a thing. Leaving the sinister dunes, she headed back towards the promenade.

5: The Tide

By the evening of the second day Gillian was convinced that the whole trip had been a mistake. She had called Aunt Emily and told her what a wonderful time she was having, feeling herself grow more and more inane as she struggled to find something to say that would break Emily's chilly silence. She had eaten in the hotel restaurant, too painfully aware of being the only person alone to enjoy her first Real French Dinner: something she had looked forward to as much as she had to wandering in the dunes. A long, long Saturday spent walking about the old town, the loud new resort and the pine woods failed to bring the anticipated sense of freedom and elation. She had expected to be afraid travelling alone, managing everything for herself, and she was; but it had never occurred to her that she might also be bored. 'The trouble with you is you've got no resources,' she said to herself among the pines. Now that she was alone, she was noticing that her inner monologue, the voice she could never remember being without, took the form of a quiet but continuous scolding in a voice very like her aunt's. Had it always been like that? Anyway, it was company of a sort.

As she entered the restaurant on the second evening, she was debating whether to stay another night and see the castle, or to move on towards Brittany. She sat down at the smallest table in the room, glanced through the menu and was just reaching into her bag for her guidebook when she became aware of someone standing just in front of her. She looked up to see a man in his mid-forties, stocky and shortish with thinning brown hair. As he was wearing a suit and most of the guests were in casual clothes, at first she thought he must be the manager, but realised her mistake when he said, 'Hi, look, please just shoot me down in flames if I'm out of order but I noticed you sitting on your own. The thing is I'm here alone, just for tonight and I'd love your company at dinner if you'll let me join you?'

He seemed so sure of himself that Gillian nodded without thinking, although at first sight she didn't much like the look of him – there was something about him, she wasn't sure what, that made her think of the bullies from her schooldays – and besides, she was trying to avoid speaking English in the hope that, after a few days, she would be immersed in French and no longer struggle to understand the simplest remark. But that seemed rather too much to explain to a stranger, and anyway it would be a relief not to be the only solitary diner again. So she gave an embarrassed smile and even offered him the menu.

'No thanks,' he waved it away, 'I'm having the platt due jaw, I asked at the door and it's seafood. Best thing about this place if you ask me.'

'Oh good,' said Gillian. She hadn't intended to ask about the dish of the day because – even if she understood the answer – she would then have felt obliged to order it no matter what it was. 'I'll have that too.'

'Great, and let me get us a bottle of wine – no, it's on me, I can claim it – let's have a look. White, I think. Hmm, don't much care for Chardonnay but … what about you?'

Barely knowing what Chardonnay was, Gillian mumbled that anything would be fine. When the waiter came her new acquaintance ordered for both of them, in a pidgin French that seemed to get a much better response than she had achieved with her precise schoolbook phrases. Still, the waiter was certainly friendlier to her now than he had been last night. His smile might have something of a leer about it, but he probably couldn't help that. She sipped her wine – even her ignorant palate could tell it was much better than the small glass of house she'd had the night before – and decided that it really was rather nice to be looked after.

As they talked, and ate, and drank, she began to feel at ease. She soon had his life story: he was called Greg, a sales rep for a furniture company, who had just finished a job in Étaples and was on his way home to Warwick next day. 'Always stay here when I'm in this neighbourhood – nice place, peace and quiet, bit of night life too if you feel like it. Do you fancy a drink in town after this?'

Why not? After a slight tussle over the bill, which she wanted to split and he insisted on paying ('I can claim it, they owe me') she let him lead her out into the streets which were now fully lit, and into a small bar where he ushered her to a stool and, without asking her, ordered cognac for them both. She was vaguely aware that he seemed to be steering her quite a lot with a hand on her behind, but after all it was dark and the floor of the bar was probably a bit uneven – she was certainly having trouble with her balance. Wobbling on her stool, she smiled dazedly at him. What a nice, considerate man he was turning out to be. It just showed that you shouldn't be too quick to judge people.

After a while she noticed that he'd stopped talking and seemed to be watching her rather closely. She forced herself to sit upright and tried to look intelligent – it would be a shame to bore him after all the trouble he had taken. 'So,' he said abruptly, 'I've gone on about myself enough, what about you? What kind of holiday is this, all on your own and out of season?'

Gillian tried to think of a way of explaining, in a few words, all the tangle of reasons that had brought her here. 'Well, you see ...' She took a deep breath and an even deeper gulp of cognac, forgetting it wasn't wine. She choked and sneezed, and then suddenly it was all beautifully clear. 'The thing is, Greg, I've never been anywhere or done anything. I've lived with my aunt all my life, really because I couldn't face up to having my own place, and all I ever do is go to work, go home, go to bed

...' Realising she was speaking faster and faster, she took another drink and went on more slowly: 'So one day I just thought, go and see the world. So I left my job and packed my bags, and well, here I am.' There! How simple everything was when you thought about it.

Greg seemed impressed. 'So you're just going to travel around until you've had enough?'

'Oh well, I couldn't afford to keep travelling for all that long; I'll have to look for another job in the end. But for a while, yes.'

'No boyfriend waiting at home?'

'Oh no, there never has been really. Even when I was at college—' but he didn't seem to be listening any more. 'You know,' he said abruptly, 'you look like you've had enough. Come on, I'll take you back to the hotel.'

Outside in the suddenly fresh wind, she did indeed feel that she'd had enough. She lurched, fell against him and was quite grateful when he put an arm round her and began to steer her back along the promenade. 'Do you know,' she said confidentially, 'yesterday I walked on those dunes over there for hours, trying to … oh, trying to feel something I suppose. Trying to feel alive, does that make any sense?'

'Sure,' Greg said absently. They were almost back at the hotel now. 'You see,' Gillian mumbled on, 'I've never really felt alive. I find everything so terrifying, Greg, I can't just seem to get on and enjoy—' She was interrupted by a sudden, hard and very wet kiss on the mouth. Too surprised to react – this sort of thing just didn't happen to her – she let herself be half led, half pulled up the stairs, and stayed leaning against him while he found his room key in the near-dark of the landing. It was past twelve now and the hotel was completely silent.

When the door opened she stumbled inside the room, and blinked around her as he snapped on the light. There was a chair by the window and, noticing that her legs were wobbly, she made her way to it and sat down heavily. Now she felt leaden and queasy and inclined to weep. When Greg came towards her, though, she found herself scrambling to her feet and launching into a feeble imitation of a guest taking polite leave of a host.

'Oh, I didn't see the time, and there you are having to leave so early in the morning, I am sorry – anyway I'll be going now, and thank you so much for—' Again, he stopped her with a slobbering kiss; this time he started to fumble at the front of her shirt as well. 'No, wait,' she muttered, turning her head to one side and pushing uselessly at the groping hands. 'That's it, sweetie, you want this, come on, that's it,' she heard as he kept on pushing.

And then all at once she was sober. 'No,' she said clearly. He paused a moment, peering into her face. She drew back, looked him in the eye and repeated, 'No.' She added, 'I'm sorry, it was the drink, I never wanted this.' He gave a muffled laugh and felt for her breasts again; this time she struck his hand away and took two steps back. His face grew dark and furious; as she made for the door he grabbed her arm, muttering something in which the word 'bitch' was all she could distinguish.

'If you don't let go of me,' said timid Gillian, 'I'm going to scream "Police", and I've got the loudest scream you've ever heard. Like to hear it now?' She took a dramatically deep breath, then let it out in a soundless pant as he hastily released her arm. He was at the door in a split second, jerked it open and pushed her through it. She heard the word 'cunt' through clenched teeth before the door closed – quietly enough, he clearly hadn't lost control – and she almost fell onto the landing.

In her own room she locked the door and collapsed on the bed, breathing so heavily that she half thought it must be audible next door. It was some time before she began to feel calmer, got up and slowly undressed while she pondered what had happened, or not happened.

It was all too easy to imagine what Kate would say. 'So let's just go through this again, Gill. This man picks you up in a hotel, insists on buying you dinner, drags you out to bars and plies you with drink, and it never occurs to you he might have a motive? How old are you, twelve?' And she would have a point, thought Gillian; naive hardly described her. Ignorant would be more accurate.

There had been one episode while she was still at school, with a boy even more awkward and derided than herself. Lonely as she was, she had still never really thought poor scrawny Stuart was the answer to anything; and he hadn't failed to let her know that she was his last, desperate choice. When she started college they both welcomed the excuse to stop meeting, and she had no idea what had happened to him after that.

Since then she'd had few dealings with men except as fellow students or work colleagues. Kate had tried to set her up once, with a balding middle manager who barely bothered to be polite and left halfway through the evening, and after that she never tried again. It just seemed easier not to start, not to battle against her terrors and try and make herself visible; even as a girl she'd never really rebelled against the way she was constrained and supervised, so differently from the others at school. At some point, she must have just accepted that she would never live as other people did; and as the years passed, trudging silently along on her treadmill of work and home, she had almost forgotten that men existed as sexual beings. That there were still those who could see *her* in that way was a genuine surprise. She wondered whether she had been in real danger; whether he actually would have raped her if she hadn't threatened him; whether, travelling alone, there might be dangers she had never experienced and scarcely even thought about. *You should be more careful*, said the internal Aunt Emily.

And yet, she thought as she slid between the cold sheets, if this had happened a month ago she would almost certainly have ended up going along with it out of sheer inability to stand up for herself. Remembering Greg's furious face and hot breath, she felt a huge relief and, very faintly, the dawning of a certain pride. She was, at long last, beginning to take care of herself; rather like Simone de Beauvoir when she jumped out of a moving car to escape an attacker, though perhaps saying 'No' in a secure hotel wasn't quite in the same league. Was this, she wondered drowsily as the bed began to warm up, what her aunt would mean by leading men on? Anyway, one thing was for sure: Emily would certainly say 'I told you so.'

In the morning she felt sluggish, feeble and sick. It was so rare for her to drink more than one glass of wine in an evening, if she drank at all, that it was a while before she recognised her symptoms for what they were. She also remembered, more clearly than she'd have wished – wasn't alcohol supposed to induce oblivion? – that she had spent the evening drinking in bars with a complete stranger, blurting out her life story and happily accompanying him to his room, before suddenly threatening him with the police. On the whole it would be simpler and less embarrassing if she left quietly before breakfast.

It was still early, not yet seven; her body was still on the British clock. She pushed back the covers and swung herself out of bed, sat for a moment with head on knees as a wave of giddiness passed over her, and then opened her laptop. She would choose a random place in Brittany, within reach of Mont St Michel, and spend a couple of days there before turning inland to explore the Loire Valley. Without taking much time to look at it – she was anxious to be gone before Greg appeared – she settled on

Ploumanach, because it had a nice-sounding name and a picture of pink rocks. There seemed to be several places to stay so she decided not to try and book in advance.

She hadn't been long on the road before she realised that if she continued to drive at this speed she was unlikely to be in Brittany before midnight. She also realised that she just wasn't ready to take it any faster: even sticking to the quietest and slowest routes, the fear that she might lose concentration and start to drive on the left was constant, while her heart still pounded unbearably every time she had to negotiate a slip road or a junction. Exhausted by the strain of imagining disaster, and weak and confused from the wine and brandy last night, she needed to take a break almost every half hour even when there was no need to consult a map. It was midday before she reached Honfleur, where, oblivious to all the charms of that town, she headed for the centre and checked into the first hotel she saw that had parking. It was cramped and unprepossessing, but Gillian had never been gladder to see anything than the brown-covered single bed in her narrow room. She bolted a salad in the nearest bistro, collapsed into the bed and slept like a stone.

She had intended to stop and visit the Mont St Michel on her way, but the next day's travelling was even more nerve-shattering than the first; and she soon knew that to reach Ploumanach in daylight was as much as she could hope for. Stopping at an aire for yet another panic break, she sat in the car and seriously asked herself what she was doing. So far she was finding the driving terrifying, the people at best unfriendly and her own company – undiluted by work or any social life at all – appallingly tedious. In her mind she began to compose an email to Kate:

You were right, this isn't for me. I've only been here three days and it feels like a month. I hate being a woman travelling alone, you're either completely invisible or a piece of meat; I don't know what I came here to do or what I was expecting to find, but ...

Seeing the words in front of her as clear as if they were up on the screen already, she abruptly deleted them. 'Who gives up after three days?' she snapped at herself, shoved the key into the ignition and set off with a lurch. She *would* go to Ploumanach – you had to have a plan and stick to it, or you would never get anywhere. She'd stay there two days no matter what, go and see whatever tourists were supposed to see and then head for the Loire. And after that ... oh, never mind, that could wait.

She got there a little after four, found a place to stay easily and as soon as she had unpacked decided to go out and look at the sea, which was little more than a hundred yards away. She had some idea that there would be a rocky shore, but that was about all. Still, it would be something to look at and she needed fresh air.

The village was more built up than she had expected, though at this season the high street showed more boarded-up shops than anything else. She hardly looked to right or left but marched along its grey length towards the beach, trying to lift her spirits by moving. The day had grown brighter and colder, and the light wind from the sea reached her at the same moment as she caught sight of the shore and stopped dead.

The rocks were huge; great bizarre shapes that could have been made of plasticine, squeezed and half moulded by some monstrous child who had tired of them and flung them down. Gillian stepped forward and gazed; they looked so soft, as if you could prod them and leave a mark, rose-coloured in the afternoon sun. She went on, slipping on vivid green seaweed. Now it was like walking among pink clouds; now like being at the foot of an immense staircase. Just across the stretch of sand where she was, she could see levels of granite shaped like steps; and following an impulse she hadn't felt since childhood, ran to the lowest point and began to climb. The stone was invitingly warm, and there were footholds; she soon found herself much higher than she'd expected. Hauling herself onto a flat surface she sat up, panting, to look out over the glittering sea, and back inland at the pine trees, and again at the sea.

It struck her that the waves seemed to be hitting the shore rather fiercely, even though the wind still wasn't strong. She looked down at the rocks she'd just climbed and wondered how she had got up so easily; getting down was going to be quite a different matter. *Well, I did warn you,* sighed Aunt Emily, just as she had done from the foot of an oak tree where the eight-year-old Gillian had got stuck and had to be rescued by a neighbour. The humiliation of that day was still with her; she had never climbed anything trickier than a stile since.

Then Auntie was drowned out by another voice, much louder, shouting, 'Madame! Madame!'

Gillian peered down and saw two figures, a man and a woman gesturing at her from the sand. Full of the middle-class British dread of trespassing, she at once began to apologise, scrambling up from her throne and almost tumbling over the edge. But the man's voice was alarmed, not angry. '*Madame, la marée vient! Il faut descendre—*'

Gillian was bewildered. '*Le ... mare? Pardon...*' She heard a muttering between the couple and then the woman called, 'The water, the – the tide! come quick.'

And now the hastily gleaned information about the Brittany coast came back to her: in the area of the Mont St Michel, the tide comes in at the speed of a galloping horse. Looking down again she saw that the sea was moving up to the bay already. She half slithered and half fell down the rocks, and her rescuers steadied her before she collapsed into the sand. Still stammering out apologies, she let them lead her away from the beach. Once safely back on the edge of the village they dusted her down, asked if she was hurt and, when she assured them that she wasn't, waved away her thanks and wandered off, arm in arm and laughing.

Gillian looked down at her jacket, smeared with what looked like pink powder, and her trousers, which were torn in several places. Grazes on her knees and forearms were beginning to smart; the soft pink plasticine was, after all, granite. She turned to look at the tide again. By now it was half way up to her plateau; a few more minutes and she'd have been marooned there or even drowned; perhaps the water covered the whole giant's toybox eventually. Standing there, chilled, battered and shaken, she was aware of an odd sensation. Everything seemed magnified – the air was so clear, she felt as though she could touch the rocks on the other side of the bay; she breathed deeply and it was as if she tasted air for the first time.

She was halfway up the street before it came to her what the feeling was. It was the sensation she had tried and failed to manufacture by pacing doggedly in the dunes at Hardelot, the thing she had been seeking when she came to France: all at once she knew that she was alive.

6: The River

Gillian stayed in Ploumanach for two days, and would have stayed longer if a school party hadn't arrived and taken over the hotel. By this time the weather had turned grey and windy again; she still felt exhilarated battling along the coast path and feeling the spray flung into her face, but heavy rain was forecast. On the other hand, everywhere around Le Mans promised to be bright and warm.

She had always felt a pull to the Loire region, and above all wanted to see Saumur, mainly because the book she had liked best from her A level French course was *Eugènie Grandet.* All she could remember now was that it was set in Saumur, but she had brought it with her and flicked through the pages as she sat by her window. The copy was an old one, and the white space of almost every page was covered with tiny blue squiggles – her own laborious translations, word for word. At first the nineteenth-century French baffled her even with the aid of her faded notes, but after a few minutes she found she was reading with ease, pleasure even. Although, looking at the opening paragraphs, it was hard to see what had made her so anxious to visit Saumur. Cold, dark, silent houses in narrow, forbidding streets; closed, repellent faces peering from behind shutters; greed and gossip and tiny, suspicious minds.

It must be the story of Eugènie that had appealed to her; a pale, wistful figure, eternally bent over her sewing, her spirit crushed by heartless adults long before she reached adolescence, and then her heart broken by her callous cousin. 'I suppose', Gillian thought, 'I enjoyed reading about someone who was having an even drearier time than I was.' She smiled at the picture of her nineteen-year-old self, bent as obediently over her set text as the heroine over her own task, and following her misfortunes with a sympathy that was surely born of self-pity, though she didn't remember seeing it that way at the time. Anyway, what had happened to Eugènie in the end? She decided to read the whole book again once she reached Saumur.

On the sixth day of her trip, she left Ploumanach early. She felt a little regret, for the place had touched something in her that she had never known existed. But for that very reason, she was anxious to get on and see more of the country, see more of life. In the end she took a meandering route, ambling along the coast to stop at the Mont St Michel and spending a night near Dinan. She was getting ever so slightly less nervous about the driving, though the thought of the autoroute was still too alarming; if she avoided that, the journey to Saumur would be about 150 miles and if she started early and took it easy, she really should be able to get there next day. For now, sleepy from sea air and new sights, she would stay peacefully in her room – funny how easily she was adapting to sleeping in different places already – and send Kate an email.

Well, it's been a week now and so far nothing terrible's happened, though better not say so I suppose. I emailed you after Hardelot so you know all about that ... well, I haven't had to defend my honour again, but even so I haven't been bored.

She paused here, thinking how unlike her it sounded – breezy, facetious even. She wondered, too, if it was strictly true. The Brittany coast and the monastery had thrilled her, and driving in France and finding accommodation was still too nerve-racking to be dull; but it couldn't be long before the novelty of single hotel rooms and the worst table in every restaurant would wear off. And just below the surface there was still that unease that had attacked her on the first day, that sense of futility. What, after all, was the point of these days spent wandering about new towns and coastal paths? If she was hoping to discover 'the real

France' she wouldn't do it this way, and if it was herself she was trying to find, well, what did that mean exactly, and how did you go about it?

Still, even to be asking these questions was progress, wasn't it? She typed on:

I'll send you some photos soon. Will you show them to Aunt Emily? I've seen some fantastic places already, and can't wait to get to the Loire Valley. And Kate, you wouldn't believe it but I'm actually enjoying the stuff I was dreading – the driving, and looking after myself generally.

Not quite true either, but she still remembered Kate's comments about her helplessness, and with the beginnings of self-reliance she was also developing an embryonic sense of pride, or face-saving; self-love, you might say. '*Amour-propre*,' she said aloud with some satisfaction. 'I really have been a bit of a doormat all my life.' Perhaps French culture was rubbing off on her after all. Her encounters with the host nationals had been limited so far, but she hadn't met a single doormat.

She added: *Hope to hear from you soon – love to Al and the kids, and if you see Aunt Emily will you tell her I'll call as soon as I reach Saumur?* and pressed Send. As soon as the email was sent she began to think how little she had told her friend of what was in her mind. It wasn't only pride, wishing to stand by her decision; after all, on the whole she was enjoying herself. But now she came to think of it she had never really confided in Kate or anyone. She had never acquired the habit of examining her sensations and comparing them with what others felt, and feminine emotional chatter bewildered her. Kate she valued for her unsentimental, if abrasive common sense and respect for Gillian's own reticence; she had no other close friend. She supposed that Aunt Emily's attitude had formed her own: 'Very nice people I expect, but let's not get too involved' was about the warmest thing she ever said of anyone outside her own narrow circle. And really,

Gillian had never got involved either, never learned the art of making friends; isolation, or what Emily called privacy, just seemed like a natural state.

So it surprised her that now, sitting with her laptop and looking out over the village square, she should suddenly long for a friend. Someone to whom she could say 'I am so lonely' and be given sympathy and understanding rather than a list of local singles clubs and evening classes.

As she travelled towards Saumur, she noticed the countryside growing gentler and, when she stopped for one of the hourly breaks she still needed, the air warmer. She began to grow impatient for a sight of the Loire itself, and of the blue roofs of the town; it was the first time on her travels that she had actually been looking forward to reaching a particular destination or even had much of a picture of one in her mind. Though no doubt Eugènie's Saumur had changed somewhat in the last hundred-odd years.

It was early afternoon when, moving at her usual slow pace along the road to Saumur, she felt the Micra begin to sputter and saw smoke in front of her. Then the car jerked, slowed right down and, just as she managed to get it onto the roadside, the engine died.

For a minute Gillian sat in the driving seat with her hands still clenched on the wheel as if she could wrench the car back into life. Then she got out and opened the bonnet and peered inside, as if anything she could do would make the slightest difference. The usual bewildering mess of wires and pipes looked back at her. She stepped back and glanced round; it was an N road, broad and straight and well signposted – she could see SAUMUR 10 KM and VIVY 2 km clearly enough – but at this time of day it was almost deserted. A car went by and then another; she lifted a tentative hand to wave for help, but lowered it again; wouldn't it be better to decide first what was needed?

There was a layby a few yards ahead. With a good deal of panting and halting, she began dragging the little car towards it, with one hand on the wheel. It was difficult to steer and push at the same time, but at last she got it to safety, put the handbrake on and sat down on the grass verge to think. So here it was, exactly the sort of situation she most dreaded; it was imagining moments like this that had always put her off travelling. Still, here she was and she must just deal with it. Her first reaction, which was to call Kate and bleat for help, was just stupid. What did a stranded driver need, with a useless vehicle and no mechanical knowledge? She could answer that one: a mechanic. Not likely to be found lurking by the roadside, though. Should she try to hitch a lift into town and look for help there? No, of course not – really Kate was right, she shouldn't be let out on her own – she must find her insurance documents, call the company and let them deal with it.

By the time she had got through to the right department, repeated her request twice and listened to a variety of holding music, her phone was very low, but the voice asking her 'Do you have breakdown insurance?' was perfectly clear.

'I, yes, I think so, I mean I think I'm covered for everything,' Gillian stammered.

'Then you'll be covered for collection of your vehicle in France. If you—' At this point the phone followed the Micra into a dead silence. More cars passed; again she half prepared to try and flag one down, but her nerve failed. In the end she locked the car and set off in the direction of the nearer town. It took more than half an hour to reach Vivy, and there was a further delay while she went into a baker's – luckily it was now after four and the siesta hour was over – asked where the nearest garage was, and bought a lemon cake she didn't want, because she felt guilty about taking up the weary-looking assistant's time for nothing.

The young mechanic was helpful enough, but Gillian soon found her French hopelessly inadequate to explain what was the matter with her car, not that she would have got much further in English. The car was not marching, it was resting beside the road about two kilometres back towards Dinan, and that was about all she could tell him. Possibly realising that she had no idea what to do, the mechanic took over, made a couple of rapid phone calls and presently announced that her car would soon be brought to the garage. Then he invited her to sit down in the gloomy office and disappeared.

It was almost six when Gillian checked into the first *pension* she could find, having been told to come back next day and see what could be done for her car. There was no internet connection, but she wrote to Kate anyway and saved the email in Drafts:

Well, here I am stranded in a village somewhere in the Loire Valley, waiting to see if I still have a car. Don't know what I'll do if they can't repair it – I suppose I could afford to buy a second-hand one, but then I'd be stuck with a left-hand drive or else have to sell it again when I come home. And it's hard enough driving with a car I know – I really don't know if I want to risk setting off in a different one. Don't say anything to Aunt E yet, will you? I'll get in touch with her as soon as I know what I'm doing.

Next morning her worst fears were realised. This time she spoke to the owner, who was a little older than the mechanic and spoke good English, though his explanation made little sense to her even so. The gist of it was that her Micra would need a new engine, and repairing it would cost more than replacing it.

'I can do this for you, Madame, but it's not recommended. However, if you decide not to repair the car it can be transported back to the UK for you and disposed of there. Can I ask if you plan to travel further in France or to return to England?'

'Well, really I was hoping to travel for a few more weeks at least,' Gillian explained hesitantly, 'but I'm not sure whether to look for another car here or not.'

'Yes, I see. Perhaps you would like to see the second-hand vehicles we have here? Please look around, I am in the office.'

Gillian thanked him and wandered off in the direction he showed her. She tried to concentrate on the Peugots and Renaults, to make some kind of judgment about what size or price she should be looking at, but she felt utterly helpless. She had reluctantly learned to drive, needing more than twice the usual number of lessons, and taken ownership of the Micra when Aunt Emily gave it up, because one of them needed to be able to use a car, but she had never chosen a vehicle in her life. How in the world was she to pick out a new one – left-hand drive at that – sort out all the paperwork, blithely hop in and set off? But the alternative was to go tamely home and … what? She was no nearer now to knowing what she wanted to do with her life than she had been a week ago. Besides, without transport she would never manage the amount of luggage she'd brought with her.

As if in a mirror, she suddenly saw herself; a drooping, defeated figure, expecting to be beaten by every little setback. No wonder she irritated people! And just as had happened on the road to Hardelot, the road to Brittany, something inside her revolted against her own cowardice. She pulled herself upright, stepped back from the line of cars and looked at her options with a new determination. She would not go home. She would go for a walk in the village and look for inspiration, and if none came – well, she would come back to the garage and just shut her eyes and pick the first vehicle that she touched, but she would not go home.

She went back into the office. 'Thank you, Monsieur, I'll come back a little later and decide.' She walked out of the gate and turned left, passing the bakery where she had bought the tart *and I only got that because I'm a coward*, and kept going until she had almost reached the end of the street.

At that point she noticed that the last house but one had a small cream-coloured camper van parked by the fence, and there was a notice on the windscreen: A VENDRE – €3000.

No, it was impossible. She must be losing her mind from all that solitary travelling and boredom; or else desperation at the idea of going back to Southash was forcing her into absurd ideas. How would she even start a thing that size, let alone take it onto a road? and anyway, was she seriously proposing to spend the coming weeks – or even months – on campsites? Yet she continued to stare at it, and presently stepped closer to peer inside. In the poor light she could make out two hard-looking sofa-like seats and a lot of narrow brown doors, and that was about all.

'Vous voulez voir le camping-car?' came a voice behind her. Gillian spun round as if she had been caught shoplifting and saw that a short, sturdy grey-haired man had come up to the gate and was looking hopefully at her. 'Certainly, Madame – this car belongs to me and my wife, but we are buying a larger one now. I have the keys inside the house – one moment, please—'

'Oh,' she began, much flustered, 'I was only looking at it, I've never driven anything like this before, and I really don't think—'

Instead of being annoyed the man seemed pleased. 'You are English?' he asked. Gillian faced what was by now a familiar dilemma: when people address you in your language in their own country, is it more polite to acknowledge their efforts by replying in the same language, or match their courtesy by using their own? But then he resolved it for her by saying, 'I study English, it is very good to practise.'

In that case it would be churlish to continue practising her French on him. She gave him an apologetic smile and turned back to the little van. 'It's very nice,' she said, 'it's just that I don't think I could drive it.'

'You have a car now?' She explained what had happened.

He looked thoughtfully at her. 'You are travelling around France, Madame, it's correct? You take a long holiday?'

'Yes, that's right. I especially wanted to see the Loire and maybe Burgundy, er, Bourgogne, but I don't have much of a plan.'

'Then a camping-car is perfect for you, isn't it? Especially this one – it's a Renault Trafic Pilote, quite small as you can see. You have freedom, you can stay at the camping for a long time and it's very cheap. And,' he was getting into his stride now, 'very convenient – usually close to the town centre. I know the English campings very well and they are not the same – not so convenient. You know, with my wife we travel all over Europe in our camping-car, and France is the best place. And for an independent traveller—'

Gillian broke in, appalled. 'But I'm not – I mean, it's very kind of you, Monsieur, but I'm a terrible driver – no really, I could hardly manage to drive my own little car …'

The owner let her stammer into silence and then said, 'You have driven here from England?'

'Well yes, of course.'

'So you have already made a long journey, driving on the right – difficult for you, I know – without any assistance or – you have satellite navigation? No? Well, you see then. Do you know, I have some friends who are experienced drivers, who refuse to rent a car in Britain because they are afraid of driving on the left? And you are travelling alone – many people, especially many women, will not do this. I think you don't need to be afraid about your abilities.'

Stunned by this new picture of herself and hopelessly drawn to the little van, Gillian gave in. 'Perhaps if I could just see inside for a moment ... ' He was in the house and back out with the keys almost before she spoke, unlocked the side door and politely motioned her in. She went up a small step, hesitated a moment and stepped inside.

Although at first it was a little dark after the brightness of the day outside, after a moment she saw that the interior was surprisingly light and airy. She was standing in what must be the kitchen, though at present she could only see cupboards and pale wooden-looking covers; she was in a space no more than two feet square, set a little lower than the rest of the van. Pulling open a cupboard door to her right she found a tiny washroom, complete with shower; turning round to the back window and lifting the covers, a two-ring gas hob and a sink which looked barely large enough to hold a teacup. With growing fascination she began to explore further; there were drawers and cupboards wherever you looked, even a little fridge and a slit of a wardrobe with a coat hanger still in it. Once up the little step she was in the seating (sleeping?) area; without thinking she dropped on to one of the narrow sofas to test it, as if in a hotel room. It was comfortable enough but surely too short to sleep on? For the first time she remembered the garage owner and looked round. He had stepped inside and was peering at a set of mysterious switches and knobs on the wall. Too entranced to be intimidated by these, Gillian demanded to be shown how the bed worked.

He showed her how a single bed could be created by using the lowered front seat on the end of one of the sofas, and a double through a complicated procedure involving the table-top, 'or you can sleep up here' – tugging at a strap that let down a huge shelf from the ceiling – 'but it won't be so comfortable for you. It's only really suitable for children.'

Still in a mood of exploration, Gillian immediately scrambled up onto the shelf – but it was not only uncomfortable, it was positively unpleasant, like being a joint of meat in a cold oven, and she soon slid down again. The single bed it would be then. It seemed that what you had to do in the morning was pull the bedding off, lift up your bed which had a big box under it, stuff the bedding inside and there was your bedroom converted back into a living room – or, as Monsieur was now enthusiastically pointing out, a dining room. 'See, you just pull out this table from behind the sofa again, and here is the …' 'Leg,' supplied Gillian, now as eager as he. 'Yes, the leg, and attach it like this, and voila! here is your table for your meals, for whatever you want. And of course, if the weather is warm you want to open this door, here, and—'

Gillian recollected herself. 'Yes, Monsieur, yes, it's a beautiful van, er, camping-car, but I really don't know if I could drive it. It looks very big and heavy for me, don't you think?'

He shook his head vigorously. No, Madame, I do not think. My wife believed the same, but she has often driven this car with no problems – wait! I will find her.'

With a beaming smile he jumped down the step and left her bewildered. Whatever was the matter with her, taking up this kind man's time, and now his wife's too, over a purchase she was never going to make? He wasn't a pushy salesman either – that was genuine enthusiasm. Now she was going to hurt his feelings by rejecting his treasure. Wasn't she?

She looked round the interior again. It was no use pretending to herself; she wanted it. She had lived all her life as a guest, a tenant, tiptoeing through her aunt's house in dread of knocking over a vase or slamming a door; and now she was still a guest, moving silently from one impersonal space to the next. This little box, this – this doll's house was something she could make her own; she could buy it this minute and sleep in it tonight if she chose.

Aren't you getting a bit carried away? croaked Aunt Emily. 'Oh, will you shut up, Auntie?' said Gillian – to her horror, aloud – just as a small, smiling woman, rather like a robin, hopped up the step and peeped inside. 'Oh, *bonjour*, Madame, er, *je* ...' But it was clear that the robin lady hadn't heard her mutterings, and anyway didn't speak English. The three of them embarked on a slightly awkward conversation, with Gillian's prim and impractical French supplemented by M. Rey's fluent but technically limited English. The essence of the conversation was that Gillian would find the Trafic perfectly easy to drive; it was all a question of going slowly and using the mirrors. Yes, she would be able to park it, it was shorter than a typical large car – 'But I've never driven a large car either' – no problem, neither had Mme Rey until they got the Trafic. Come, she could at least sit in the driving seat and see how it felt ...

As soon as she sat behind the wheel, Gillian knew that she was in love. She was so high up, with such a fantastic open view, and looking at the pedals and controls it was reassuring to see that most of them were recognisably the same as in any other car. She had been half expecting something along the lines of an aeroplane cockpit. She looked back at the expectant Reys and said, 'Well ...perhaps I could try just a little drive?'

M. Rey was in the passenger seat almost before she had finished the question, and his wife bounced down just behind Gillian and peered over her shoulder. Gillian was so terrified, she was sure she must be breathing loudly enough for them both to notice. She pressed her back against the seat and shifted her hands on the wheel, breathing slowly and deeply for a few moments. Then she smiled apologetically and said, 'I'm very nervous – I will need to go very, very slowly.' Any hint of a Gallic sneer and she would have been out of the cab and away, but they only nodded in understanding.

'*Absolument,*' agreed Madame. 'Or', suggested Monsieur, 'if I drive at first? I can drive to a bigger place, and then you can start as slowly as you like.' Gillian accepted gratefully, they changed places and she watched closely as he started the engine, changed into first gear with a rather hefty push and gently began to steer towards the gateway. Except for the bigger scale, really it did all look much the same as her own Micra. In fact, watching his hands on the wheel she was conscious of a very faint, dawning sense of territory. 'Give me that, it's mine,' something in her seemed to be saying.

When they reached a quiet back road, they changed places again. This time she went straight for the wheel and let in the clutch almost without thinking. Everything felt huge and cumbersome, but not unmanageable. Using the mirrors was odd – there was a moment of alarm before she worked them out; nevertheless, that new sensation of ownership didn't wear off. And to be in a left-hand drive vehicle, after the Micra, made more difference than she would have believed; for the first time, driving on the right felt natural. She inched up to the next junction and, following slightly conflicting instructions from the Reys, steadily carried the three of them back to the garage, where her hosts gave her a largely incomprehensible lecture on hooking up, using the gas and the mysteries of the chemical toilet, and gave soothing answers to her questions about insurance and the forest of paperwork she was sure would be needed. It was all easy, they would arrange everything, Madame should not disturb herself.

In the end it was agreed that she should hire the van for the weekend. She paid a deposit, accepted a scrawled sheet of directions to the Camping Municipal de Saumur and set off about eleven o'clock. Finding Saumur wasn't difficult, and nor was locating the campsite as it was clearly marked by those prominent brown caravan and tent signs which she had often seen but never paid any attention to. It was a vast place – she had imagined a field with a few tents and vehicles dotted about on the grass, but it was more like an entertainment complex with tennis courts and a swimming pool. Most of the facilities seemed closed, but to her relief reception was open, and she made her booking without difficulty. It was when she tried to get onto her chosen pitch that things began to get tricky. Backing the monster onto the generous square of concrete wasn't too bad, but when she stopped the engine and got out she found that she had parked – no, pitched – the wrong way round and wouldn't be able to reach any of the electric points. So she had to get back in, turn round and do the whole manoeuvre again, this time almost crushing two Dutch women who were cycling past. Luckily, they didn't seem to mind but hung around shouting out helpful advice. In the end one of them actually jumped up into the cab and helped her to site the van, waving away her embarrassed thanks and explanations.

When at last she was established on her new pitch – her *emplacement*, she must remember that – Gillian looked around the site with both pride and alarm. Here she was, with her very own home for the first time in her life, and if it wasn't exactly the home most people dreamed of, it was just right for her. The pitch had its own water tap and electric point, and after some hunting she managed to find the coiled electric cable, and the plug-in point hidden behind a little door on the outside of the van. And now she had electricity and water, just like in a real house, and no doubt after a few more hours' study of the manual, the weird array of switches would all make perfect sense.

Besides, she had the Reys' mobile number in case anything went seriously wrong.

On the other hand, she was now tethered, by a long lead, to a very large field in a country she hardly knew, on the edge of a town she knew not at all except through a work of fiction more than 150 years old. She was starting singlehanded on a lifestyle that she knew only as the butt of jokes – the preserve of the elderly, the staid and the very sad. 'So I should fit right in,' she remarked to the non-existent neighbour on her right. She'd chosen a part of the site that seemed almost deserted, hoping to have some peace and few witnesses while she fumbled her way around.

Anyway, here she was, hungry, thirsty and beginning to feel the heat; even though it wasn't yet May, the afternoon sun was strong. She rummaged under one of the seats, found the handle and began to tug feebly at the awning, which had opened up so beautifully for Mme Rey, but it only groaned. After a couple of pulls she gave up, terrified of breaking the whole thing, and retreated inside to think. Clearly, this lifestyle took a lot of planning. In the first place she had no food supplies of any kind, and what did you do in the evenings? But after the days spent feeling self-conscious in hotels or driving nervously on strange roads, this silent solitude was bliss. Forgetting her thirst, she leaned back against the thin wall and closed her eyes.

7: The Town of Blue

Gillian was woken before seven by birdsong, so loud that for a moment she believed she was back in Aunt Emily's house. Once she remembered where she was she lay back, stretching out as comfortably as the odd ridges in the bed would allow, and thought over the previous day. After the triumph of getting the gas and electricity to work, the excitement of pressing switches and seeing real lights come on, she had done no more than look around the site; the beauty of the town, glimpsed across the river that almost touched the site, at that point seemed more than she could deal with. She found that the site had a little shop-café which luckily was open, and having found some skimpy tagged teabags and swallowed a plate of frites, retreated to her new home to sit beside the open side doors until the river breeze grew too chilly. After that she stayed inside reading *Eugènie Grandet* until it was time for the ordeal of learning to make the bed. Bits fell down and trapped her fingers, and other bits went missing and had to be unearthed from the cupboards. Then the bedding proved strangely intractable; it didn't like being squashed into a box under a seat, and it took all her strength to drag it out. 'You're a weakling,' she remarked as she sat back on the floor and rested, 'do you good to have to do some manual work after being waited on all this last week.'

Exhausted by the day's events, she had slept as deeply as she could ever remember doing, waking only once to find herself being watched by evil red and green eyes. She lay absolutely still, a familiar terror taking over, until that new, bolder voice that she had begun to notice lately pointed out that these were, in fact, the electricity indicator lights above the fridge and that all she had to do was hang a tea towel over them.

Which meant she would have to buy a tea towel. And a bath towel, come to think of it. Not to mention cooking utensils – kind Mme Rey had left her a saucepan and some odd bits of cutlery, but for what might well be several months' living (for there was no question in her mind – she would buy the van as soon as the garage opened on Monday) more would be needed. There was a lot to do; full of energy now, she jumped out of the lumpy bed, making the whole van rock, and fished under it for her clothes, which felt and smelt slightly damp. Making the bed back into a sofa was easier than the other way round, and before eight she was off the site and heading for the bridge that joined the campsite to the town.

The first clear sight of Saumur pulled her up short. It was her first moment close to the Loire, and nothing she had read or heard had prepared her for the breadth and calm of the river, or the impact of the chateau reflected in it. She stood halfway over the bridge, lost in amazement until she was nearly knocked into the road by a speeding bike. Moving slowly on, she remembered the other reason she'd wanted to see Saumur: a French assistant at her school had described it once as 'the town of blue' and for some reason that picture had stayed with her ever since. What else had Évelyne said? 'The Loire is not a blue river; rather it is grey and green, from the trees reflected in it.' The town of blue, grey and green …yes, it made sense. There were the blue-grey slate roofs of the houses, unchanged surely since long before Eugènie's time; there was the misty green of the riverside willows that seemed to melt into the water.

Crossing into the town, she was aware of a wistful feeling that she couldn't define, something new and yet deeply familiar; she stayed for a while on the riverbank, looking back at the grey and green expanse and trying to pin down the feeling. It eluded her, so she turned towards the turreted and cobbled centre. As she wandered through the streets she noticed that although they were still quiet – it was barely eight – there were stalls piled with fruit and vegetables, splashes of bright fabric and glass jewellery in all colours. She saw chickens on spits ready to start roasting and, remembering that she'd had no breakfast, bought herself a stuffed baguette from another stall and sat down on a bench with it to watch the stallholders and the first desultory shoppers. The wistfulness was still there, growing stronger as she slowly consumed her sandwich a l'americaine; she wandered into a café on the edge of the square, ordered a large coffee and continued to ponder.

It wasn't until she had drunk her coffee and was about to pay that she managed to identify what was in her mind. It was a sense – not of homecoming, but of home itself; the *idea* of home. It wasn't that Saumur felt like home, or that France itself did; but somehow, slipping unnoticed through the quiet streets of this ancient town, she was beginning to understand that she need not always live like a ghost. She needn't always creep into a room as if she had no right to be in it, inhabit every place as if she were an unwelcome visitor who might be ordered to leave at any moment. 'I could have a home of my own,' Gillian thought, looking out through the window of the dark café. All the people who had lived in those tall dark houses, just like the Grandet house – they had all had lives, had been people. Even the people like herself and Eugènie, the ones who were always alone, went out into the world, touched other lives, made their mark in ways large or small.

Then she remembered that she already had a home of her own – fifteen feet long, self-contained and able to be set down anywhere in the world – or at least, given its age and the standard of her driving, anywhere within a few hundred miles. What limitless freedom for one who had moved for over thirty years in a caged wheel of routine, all within a circle no larger than a day's walk. She got up, full of excitement, and went to the counter to pay the waitress, whose boredom wasn't noticeably lessened by her only customer's radiant smile and unreasonably large tip.

Outside Saumur was waking up to a pale spring morning. Soon Gillian was having to dodge the market-day crowds as she wandered past stalls and shops, losing the way back and finding it again, looking and listening and smelling the food and river smells, feeling as if her senses themselves were something newly gained. She imagined that she was Eugènie Grandet herself, escaped from her silent narrow house and her monstrous, miserly father, exploring for the first time the streets that ran outside her high window, savouring the world that had been denied her. She almost shivered as she imagined how it would be to have all this snatched away again; to be forced back into the dark house, the cold room and the piles of waiting work.

All the same, you couldn't just wander around all day thinking 'Freedom!', could you? After a while she remembered that she was now a householder, like other visitors to the market; she had errands. The rest of the morning passed happily in finding pans and other necessities for the van. Getting everything she needed took the best part of the day, leaving no time for the compulsory visit to the chateau.

That evening, with a dolls'-tea party sense of occasion and a little nervousness about the sputtering gas rings, she carefully cooked the chicken leg, potatoes and green beans she had bought in the town and sat down at her assembled table. She'd need a picnic table and chairs next, so she could eat outside when the summer got going, though it was really quite warm already. After dinner and the half-task, half-game of washing up her dishes in the tiny sink, she went for another walk round the site, idly planning her next move. Once everything was arranged with the Reys on Monday, would she stay in Saumur or move on along the Loire? And where should she go after that?

'Excuse me,' said a voice from out of the dusk, 'aren't you English?' Gillian was alarmed for a moment, but then a stout elderly couple stepped from out of the shadows, and she recognised one of them as a woman who had greeted her on the way to the shower blocks yesterday. She admitted it, and within minutes found herself being dragged back to their huge motorhome and forced to have a glass of beer beside it. They introduced themselves as Phil and Maureen, gave her a long account of their travels illustrated by wads of seemingly identical photographs, and demanded that she do the same for them. What was she doing here all alone?

'I, er, just wanted to see France and do some travelling,' Gillian uttered, thinking how unconvincing it sounded. 'All on your own?' Maureen peered into her face suspiciously. 'You're a brave girl, aren't you? You wouldn't get me staying in a 'van on my own even in England, let alone abroad. Aren't you worried about all those thieves who creep into motorhomes at night and gas them?'

Gillian was startled. 'What thieves? What kind of gas?'

'I don't know what kind, dear, but it's well known. They break in while you're asleep, seal up all the vents and it puts you out so you don't hear a thing until you wake up.'

'They don't seal the vents,' Phil said impatiently, 'they pour the gas in *through* the vents. And then—'

'Seal up is what I heard.'

They seemed ready to bicker for the rest of the evening, so to distract them Gillian asked if they'd ever known anyone who got gassed. They hadn't, but friends of friends … She decided not to set them off quarrelling by pressing for more details, but to ask the Reys on Monday if they knew anything about this menace. Or would they deny there was any danger because they wanted her to buy the van? No, they were honest people, there was really no doubt.

That night, for the first time since leaving Southash the night terrors came back, as the excitement of the last two days gave way to her default condition of anxiety. Still not used to sleeping in the van, she kept sitting up in a sweat, trying to identify its odd creaks and scrapes and to be sure that none of them was anything like the sound of a gas-bearing intruder. In the end she found the light and put it on, and lay looking at the soft greyish ceiling, telling herself that the roof vent wasn't moving and that the darker shadows in the corners weren't huge crouching spiders. But it was too unnerving, lying in the dark in a big box with all that unknown land and water outside; after a while she rolled herself off the bed and, as she had done early that morning, gingerly lifted the lid off the hob, lit the gas at the third attempt and slowly boiled water in the saucepan to make herself some tea. Now, though, the pleasure of doing this was gone. What was she doing, setting off in this rattling bucket to sleep in fields and laybys and probably get herself murdered? or if she escaped a melodramatic end – back in bed now and sipping her drink, her imagination began to calm down somewhat – at any rate to have to deal with breakdowns and horrible parking manoeuvres? Not to mention the question of whether campsite life was for her. The stares she had encountered as she tried to pitch the van yesterday suddenly, in memory, seemed hostile and almost frightening; on the other hand there was the truly frightening prospect of being befriended by more Phils and Maureens everywhere she went. And finally: where exactly did she want to go, and why?

She woke next day feeling empty and depressed, even worse than she'd felt the day after the encounter with Greg. At least then she'd had her escape to arrange, as well as the satisfaction of having stood up for herself for once. Now she was stuck here for the day, too tired to enjoy exploring the town of blue and too unsure of her goals to make any more plans. Maybe she should call the Reys and tell them she wouldn't be buying the van after all? Call the Reys ... she'd never charged her phone after it died on the road along with the Micra. She got up and dressed – yes, definitely a bit damp – went through the rigmarole of rearranging the bed and fished the phone out of the bag. Then there was a scramble through the case that was still perching on the shelf-bed to find the charger, which had separated from the adaptor, then finding a plug and leaving it to charge – only to find, when she checked it a little later, that the phone wasn't only flat but actually dead. Of course it was an old one and very basic; she'd never really had much use for a phone, and only got one so Aunt Emily could reach her in an emergency. Clutching it now and staring at its blank face, she remembered Kate saying, 'Will your phone hold out, Gillian? Shouldn't you get a new one?' much as she'd said about the Micra.

So now she had that to think about as well. Could she even buy a phone in France? What did people do? Everything seemed to be telling her that it was time to give up this silliness and go home, and find another job in another windowless office and crouch in front of another screen.

To try and lift her mood she wandered over to the site café, ordered a coffee and croissant and sat listlessly down at a table on the terrace. The weather was warm and rather muggy; she supposed she'd go to see the chateau and then decide what she was going to do on Monday. She had finished the croissant and was just starting on her coffee when she noticed the Dutch couple she had nearly knocked off their bikes when she arrived, and who'd helped her to pitch up. She waved, and on an unusual impulse offered to buy them coffee as thanks for their help. They accepted readily and as always when expected to socialise, she had a moment of dismay, but they were relaxed, friendly people and quite ready to sit and chat about the Loire,

France in general and campsite life. Unlike Maureen and Phil they didn't seem to think she was odd or 'brave' to be travelling on her own; it soon emerged that they had been all over Europe and America, hiking and sleeping in tents, both separately and together; and that the lifestyle which to Gillian was a dizzying adventure, to them was a sedate and comfortable form of relaxation, suited to their middle years.

Remembering the story which had kept her awake the night before, she asked them about the gas marauders. They both shouted with laughter. 'Oh Gillian, that's an old story,' said Marije. 'Haven't you heard it? People put these rumours on the internet and then everyone believes them.'

'Think about it,' said Sanne. 'Where do you get this gas that makes you unconscious but never kills anyone? I'm sure the police would love to know how it's made.'

'But people have …'

'People have drunk too much, gone to bed and been robbed. That happens for sure. And then they think, oh, I must have been gassed, that's why I didn't hear anything.'

'And of course it sounds better on the insurance claim,' added Marije. 'Better than "I got drunk and forgot to lock the doors"!'

Gillian felt both foolish and wonderfully relieved. It would be a lesson to her, she decided, to think for herself in future and not believe everything she was told – another aspect of Aunt Emily's training that she would have to shake off. She smiled at her new friends, suddenly feeling as light and carefree as if the coffee were champagne.

'So what are your plans now?' asked Sanne.

'I'm not sure, except for seeing more of the Loire while I'm here. I'm not used to travelling, you know, or making plans.'

They both looked thoughtful for a moment. Then Marije said, 'What is it you want, really?' When Gillian hesitated she added, 'You don't need to answer; I know we Dutch are more direct than you English.'

'No, no, it's a good question, it's just …' What did she want? She remembered her drunken attempt to explain the same thing to Greg. What had she said to him? 'I've never really lived.' What did that even mean?

She looked down at her cup and then at Marije. 'I suppose I'm not sure what I want. I seem to have done what other people expected me to, ever since I can remember.'

Sanne nodded. 'It's a very good idea then, what you're doing now. You need time to think. And if you get a little scared or a little bored, what does it matter? Time – nobody has time any more. You're still young, you can do anything you want.'

Gillian smiled at them both. 'You're right – time is the best thing you can have.' And, she thought as she made her way back to her van a little later, it was true that she was still young, or young enough. All of a sudden she *felt* young.

8: History

On her last day in Saumur, after wasting the morning trying to force herself to call Aunt Emily, Gillian wrote to her instead. As briefly as possible she told her about the car and the camper van, explained she would be moving about for a few days and promised to phone soon. She meant to email Kate, but in the end, when she went to the post office for a stamp she got a phone card as well. She would call Kate from a box that evening, putting off the nuisance of getting another phone. They hadn't spoken since she arrived in Ploumanach, and so far Gillian had ducked out of emailing her about the van. To delay telling her any longer would be both unfriendly and slightly weird; the sort of behaviour that might lead to a cross-channel rescue attempt.

'So,' said Kate, 'what are you up to now? Where are you exactly?'

Gillian felt herself smiling. 'I'm in a phone box in Saumur, that's on the Loire, and I'm staying at a campsite.'

'What? Whatever are you doing at a campsite?'

'Well, the thing is I've bought a camper van.' She hurried on, over the astonished splutterings at the other end, 'You see my car broke down – yes, yes, I know you told me it would never make it, well it didn't – and then I found this lovely little Renault Trafic for sale, and I thought why not? It's awesome, Kate, I'll send you some pictures—'

'Do you mean,' Kate managed to break in, 'that you're driving yourself around France in an old camper van? and sleeping on campsites?'

Gillian giggled. 'You make it sound like something illegal, why shouldn't I? Actually it's not that hard to drive, and the people here are lovely, they all help—'

'You know,' said Kate, you don't sound like yourself at all. Are you sure you're all right?'

Gillian felt slightly deflated. She was more than all right, couldn't her friend hear how much she was enjoying herself? 'Oh, I'm fine, I've never had so much fun in my life,' she said, but now she suspected that to Kate, rather than just happy, she sounded hysterical or desperate; a relentlessly jolly spinster touring Europe because she didn't have a life to go back to. Still, that was an advance on being seen as a dull and lonely spinster living with her maiden aunt because she was afraid to go out and see the world. She went on, trying to sound super-sensible, 'It's doing me the world of good, getting out of my comfort zone.' Kate liked management-speak.

'Well,' Kate's voice was dubious, 'as long as you're happy ... so how long are you going to stay in France now?'

'I'm not sure, but at least a couple of months if I can afford it. Mind you, these sites are so cheap, and' – she had no idea she was going to say this until the words came out – 'I was thinking I might try and write a bit in the evenings. You know, a sort of journal or a blog, Englishwoman travelling in France – I could even get something published, who knows?' And once she'd said it, it was like the night she had woken up and decided to go to France: as if someone else were telling her what to do, and she had no choice but to obey.

'Anyway,' she hurried on, before Kate could start probing, 'how about you? Is Al all right, and Martha and Jack?'

'Yes, yes, we're all fine.'

'And Aunt Emily? I've written to her and I'll call as well, but you know she never really says anything about how she is.'

'Yes ... she's OK.' It seemed to Gillian that there was a slight hesitation in Kate's voice, but it was hard to be sure with the traffic noises outside and the evening was growing colder and darker, so she said heartily, 'Great, that's great. Well, say hello to everyone for me and I'll email again when I get to Chinon.'

Again there was a brief pause. 'Yes of course. Well, enjoy yourself, Gill.'

On the way back to the site Gillian wondered whether she'd imagined that hint of unease. Was it just that, as she became a little less preoccupied with her own anxieties, she noticed a vulnerability in others for the first time?

All the same, when she set off next morning she realised that she still had plenty to be anxious about. Packing up was a fraught enterprise when everything had to be secured so carefully; the number of cables and leads attached to the van seemed to have multiplied since her kind friends – now nowhere to be seen – had helped her to connect them; and when she did manage to drive off, she had to pull up sharply when the milk carton fell out of the fridge because she hadn't fixed the door shut with a locking pin as she'd been told. A few yards further on she had to stop again, to inspect the mysterious rattling noises that seemed to be coming from everywhere at once.

Pulling away from the site and onto the road seemed much harder than driving there had been on Friday. She wondered if she'd been high with excitement that day; now there was a very Mondayish terror in the sensation of all that vehicle bulking behind her, and the slow heavy movement of the gears. As she peered over the wheel to see if the road was clear, she had a moment's regret for her neat little Micra. Then the road cleared, she pulled cautiously out and, puttering along the quiet roads, empty now of rush-hour traffic, began to feel rather majestic, as if she were riding an elephant. This lasted until the elephant had to lurch to a halt when she failed to notice a red light until the last moment. After this she grew cautious again, finally crawling into the Rey drive well after eleven.

They seemed delighted to see her, and when she told them she wanted to buy the van had to be dissuaded from celebrating her new nomad status with a little aperitif. She was pretty sure that what mastery she had over the van wouldn't survive even a tiny amount of alcohol. But still shaken by the drive and the thought of what she was doing, she gratefully accepted a cup of coffee and an invitation to sit down and tell them about her plans, and explained that she wanted to go to Chinon next and then spend some weeks exploring the valley.

She'd mainly fixed on Chinon as being only a short drive from Saumur and, according to her internet research, having a nice handy campsite. At the moment that was probably about all she could manage; but she had an idea that something historic had taken place there – something to do with Joan of Arc, perhaps? She asked the Reys, but like natives everywhere they were vague about their region's history. However, they did assure her that there were some interesting wine cellars and a fine view from the inevitable chateau.

'And the holiday season has not started, so you will be very quiet and not disturbed. Chinon is very popular with British tourists, but not at this time of year. This is a very good time to visit the Loire Valley, before the hot weather.'

They didn't have internet banking, so M. Rey gave her a lift to the bank to arrange a transfer, and then there were the documents to be handed over and some more last-minute advice, most of which she couldn't follow. It was afternoon when she clambered back into the cab and was waved off, feeling as if she were the Reys' teenage daughter leaving home for the first time, and hoping she wouldn't disappoint them.

Settling into the municipal campsite was much easier in Chinon than in Saumur, and this time she paid more attention to her surroundings, not heading for the most isolated pitch but securing one with a clear view of the river. She still had to fumble around to find the leads for the hook-ups, and found it very hard to decide when the van was on level ground – even after using M. Rey's trick of rolling a coin on a surface to see if it fell off – but it wasn't long before she was sitting under the awning on one of the spindly plastic chairs the Reys had bequeathed her, looking across at the Loire – no, this was the Vienne, she must remember that too – and planning the rest of the day. The idea that had come to her yesterday, of writing about her travels, might have started as a defence against Kate's disapproval, but it wasn't the first time she had ever felt the urge to write. As a solitary child she had never been without a stub of pencil for writing down her imaginary adventures and then, in the silliness of adolescence, had solemnly recorded her profound insights for posterity. And one day Aunt Emily had found her diary and told her what she thought of it, and since then Gillian had never written a word except for work and emails.

But now it was as if she had been waiting for this: the way you can go hours without thinking of food, but at the sight and smell of it be suddenly overwhelmed with hunger. She might start a blog sometime; or she might try writing articles for the motorhome magazines she'd seen in the petrol stations. Meanwhile, she would sit on peaceful evenings and scribble, or type if she had that much to say, and then at least she would have a record of her, her ... journey? holiday? escape?

She made a start that evening, after her first foraging expedition into the town.

Chinon is a peaceful small town of about 10,000 inhabitants. Accurate, but hardly likely to thrill.

On first catching sight of the Chateau de Chinon towering above the town ... Too solemn and gushing. Clearly this writing business wasn't going to be easy.

Perhaps it would be better to decide who she was writing *for?*

She made a few more unsatisfactory attempts, gave up for the moment and poured herself a glass of wine. It was a Loire Valley rosé; she still knew nothing about wine, but this one seemed very delicious. She sat sipping, gazing out through the open window at the darkening river and thinking idly of vineyards, and wine harvests, and all the generations who had lived here, and tended grapes and made wine, and drunk it, and gone on with the business of living. Would she ever have the equivalent of a vineyard, or a patch of land – something her own, that would need her; something that would make a difference to the world, however small?

In a slightly maudlin mood, she reached for the cheap biro and child's notebook that she'd bought that afternoon and began to scribble, with no idea of what she was going to write until she wrote it.

I'm a single thirtysomething (clichés so soon? Change later) *woman with no family.* (Wasn't that unfair to Aunt Emily? Never mind, worry about that later.) *Until a few weeks ago I was stuck in a pointless job with no idea what I was doing there, and no life outside work either. As I write this, I am sitting in a small camper van on a riverside campsite, in the Loire region of France. This van is my only home at present. I have no idea what I'll be doing this time next week. How did I get here? and what happens next?*

Yes, a sort of diary would be best. She could decide later what to do with it. More contentedly now, she continued:

I'm not a courageous person. I'm very nervous about meeting people and I never know what to do in an emergency – in fact I struggle with quite everyday situations.

I'd never been abroad before in my life, and I'm still not sure what made me decide to come on this journey, except that I realised I needed to go somewhere I couldn't fall back on routine; where there was no one to tell me what to do or make decisions for me.

The first day was terrifying; I'm a hopeless driver, in fact I avoid the motorways even at home. But I set off in my car…

Or would that be confusing, as she'd already mentioned the camper van? Never mind that either, the main thing was to get started. She chewed the end of the pen and leaned back with closed eyes for a while, letting the last few weeks drift through her mind. The indifferent farewells at the office; the panic attacks on the way to the tunnel; the dunes at Hardelot; then Plumanach and the shock of beauty … She began to write again, faster and faster as the memories crowded in.

Next day Gillian booked a week at the campsite. She was beginning to want to spend time in a single place, and there was something about Chinon, even more than Saumur, which attracted her. On the second day she bought a guide to the town and earnestly made her way through it; after that she set off on tours of the places recommended in it. Once she'd got a good idea of the town she would have a go at writing something more structured.

Her neighbours seemed to be mostly middle-aged and elderly couples, mainly French, with a fairly even mix of British and Dutch and a few Germans. The children, probably grandchildren in a lot of cases, were very small, too young for school. After a day or two she began to exchange greetings with some of the friendlier people, but there were no more Phils and Maureens; time passed in a busy solitude. Now that she had a purpose, the days moved more quickly than they had ever done in her life. She visited Rabelais' birthplace, the chapel of St Radegonde and a wine-tasting cellar. Every evening after her excursions she wrote notes, using her laptop now and cheating with information from the internet if any details were hazy. They often were, and not only after the visit to the wine cellars; she had decided to take only French-speaking tours, and although she was slowly improving, as often as not she had to guess a large part of what the guides were saying.

On the Friday after her arrival in Chinon, she made her way up through a jumble of streets to the chateau. Several people had told her 'it would be much better in a year or two' when the restoration work was completed, but that seemed a rather long time to wait and she wanted to write about it. Skipping the guided tour, she found her own way around. She stayed for a long time looking at the family tree of Henry of Anjou, trying to assimilate the fact that this was the same Henry II that she could just remember reading about. So the father of Richard Lionheart and John Lackland had lived here, where she was standing, walked on these ramparts and spiral staircases where groups of schoolchildren were even now being herded. It didn't feel real; it was even harder, staring at the great tapestry and then standing in the tower that housed the Joan of Arc museum, to make herself believe that yes, this woman had existed; not as a kind of semi-mythical Robin Hood figure, but a flesh-and-blood human like herself and the schoolchildren.

But when she reached the top of the bell tower it did become real. She felt, for the first time in her life, a moment of connection; of herself, an insignificant tourist, as a part of the long human story. I'm here, she thought, as Jeanne was here, and Eleanor; she held on to the edge of the parapet and gazed and gazed. It was a *feminine* landscape; she could think of no other word to describe that gracious sweep of river vanishing into distant fields, the mellow shapes of old houses and the stretch of vineyards. It was easy to imagine that those scheming, magnificent women could have looked out over this and thought: mine, mine ...

Going back down the spiral stairs and the hill into the town, she found her mind still full of the day's visions, as if the river and the hills had become part of her. As she fell asleep that night the river seemed to be flowing past her open window, and she drifted onto it and was carried out into the heart of the valley.

9: Omelette and Apple Pie

When Gillian's week at the site was up she booked another. By now it was mid-May and the days were warm, by British standards almost hot, although the local people she met were still wearing their coats and complaining of chilly winds. She was starting to be greeted in the smaller shops when she went to buy bread or groceries, and sometimes chatted with the site wardens; it was still frustrating to have to work so hard to understand a conversation, when reading was already relatively easy, but over the days it began to get better. She had almost finished writing a description of Chinon; perhaps it was time to move further east along the Loire or even to go further south. But the ancient town still held her; she decided she would stay a little longer, maybe get some books and learn more about the whole region before choosing a new place.

On market day it was hot, even before ten o'clock when she went to the Place Jeanne d'Arc to get ideas for her article and something tasty for dinner. She was heading for a cheese stall when her eye was distracted by a flash of bright blue; changing direction, she found herself standing in front of a row of light cotton dresses hanging from a high railing. There was nobody else looking, for only a mad English tourist would be thinking about summer clothes in May.

There were all the primary colours, and jade and orange and shocking pink, as well as more subdued greys and lilacs. Gillian looked down at herself; with all the changes that had been taking place in her life, she had never given a thought to her appearance until this moment, and had travelled all through Brittany and the Loire Valley in the neat black trousers and sensible skirts that she had been wearing all her adult life, sticking to drab colours and loose fits. At the moment she was wearing a dark grey pleated skirt and baggy top so dreary that even Aunt Emily couldn't possibly have accused her of drawing attention to herself. Without any conscious thought she seized the peacock-blue dress that had first attracted her, unhooked it and called out to the stallholder, 'Can I try it on?'

He showed her into a sort of roofless tent at the back, made from hanging draperies, and she scrambled out of her clothes and into the dress in seconds. Usually desperately self-conscious in front of shop assistants, she pushed her way straight out again to look for a mirror, and found one leaning at an awkward angle against the side of the stall. '*Très belle, Madame,*' lied the stallholder as she peered into it. The dress was garish, ill-fitting and would probably be reduced to a rag after one wash; Gillian paid for it at once and walked out of the market square wearing it, with her good quality skirt and blouse stuffed into a carrier bag. The sun was on her thin arms and legs and she felt childishly happy.

Back at the site, she finished her article within an hour, spent another hour or two googling motorhome and caravan magazines, and once she had found half a dozen emailed it off to all of them. In the afternoon she was preparing to set off again, with the British traveller's guilt-driven need to be out and doing as long as the sun shone; but she found herself lingering. Whether it was the effect of sending the article, or the blue dress, or the warm air and the light over the water, she felt like a different person today, as if her voice would sound like someone else's if she spoke aloud. And in the dingy mirror at the stall this morning, it had almost seemed that she *saw* another person, not the drooping, pallid image she was used to but a stranger: skin coloured by the spring sun, dark hair thicker, eyes brighter.

For the first time since she got her passport she thought of her real name. Perhaps it was time to start using it: with a new name, it must be easier to feel like a new self. As she'd done on her first evening in Chinon, she reached for a piece of paper, with no idea what she wanted to put on it, and wrote: *My name is Ghislaine, but I've been called Gillian all my life.*

She read the words and instantly crossed them out, feeling herself flushing scarlet as if someone had overheard her speak them aloud – how self-centred, how trivial – crumpled the paper, closed up the van and went to walk along the half-island that stretched from the other side of the bridge. But the feeling wouldn't be walked away. When she came back in the late afternoon, the scolding voice that was never out of her head for long was still at war with this other one, the one that was urging her to commit the cardinal sin of *talking about herself*. And so she sat on the warm grass that sloped down towards the river, took off her shoes and stayed looking out over the water and listening to the new voice.

I've been called Gillian all my life, but my name is Ghislaine. I was given this name by my mother, a Francophile and, as I like to picture her, a romantic. I don't know for sure though, because she died in a ferry accident when I was very small; so my name is all I have from her. About my father I really don't know anything at all. I understand even my mother wasn't sure who he was, but the whole story is very ...' Murky? Fragmented? Aunt Emma's distaste for what she called 'unpleasant subjects' had made it very hard for her to explain, in language intelligible to a child, that her niece was the product of a drunken fling, but that seemed to be more or less the truth.

I'm called Gillian because my Aunt Emily doesn't believe in silly foreign names. Aunt Emily is my mother's older sister, and I've lived with her all my life. I've always called her Aunt Emily, because she doesn't believe in silly pet names either.

She let the pen drop, rolled onto her stomach and lay propped on her forearms, digging her toes into the grass to feel the slight dampness of the earth. Even this was freedom, lying like this with no one to ask what you were doing or nag you into doing something else. Just lie like this and remember.

It was her first day at school:

'Jis – er, Jisslaine?' The teacher looked from the register to the rows of waiting faces and back again. 'Giz…lane – Bailie?' At the last word Gillian very slowly put up a hand. The teacher peered at her. 'I thought Auntie said your name was Gillian, dear?' Gillian could only stare at her. How could her name have vanished, to be replaced by this weird collection of sounds that even all-knowing Miss could do nothing with? As she continued to stare in silence, the girl nearest to her began to snigger, and one by one they all joined in.

'GIZZ-lane, JIZZ-lane, can't say HER name' was a popular chant for only a few days, though ruder variations of it would reappear from time to time when they all grew older, but her place outside the group was fixed from that day. There were too many other oddities: the way she lived, not with either parent but with a remote being always referred to as 'Aunt Emily'; her old-fashioned clothes; the prissy, over-precise way she was taught to speak; the way she was kept apart.

She couldn't remember thinking about all this before. It was just another part of the way things were: the world was alien and hostile, and she didn't fit into it. How odd, though, that she should have managed to forget that day so completely; and yet, she supposed, that was the reason she never said her name aloud unless forced to for some official purpose. Even Kate didn't know it.

Well, she might write about all that one day. But now what she wanted was a snapshot: a life in a page. Which shouldn't be hard, since few lives could have contained less variety. Or have been less examined; how was it, for instance, that for all intents and purposes she'd managed to forget, literally, her own name?

However 'unpleasant' the circumstances may have been, I've always had the impression that she wasn't too sorry to have her suspicions confirmed about the kind of lifestyle young Rose had been enjoying ever since she got away from their parents. Of course, young Rose was over thirty when she produced me, but I imagine both Emily and my grandparents still saw her as a wayward teenager. That's certainly how Emily still sees me – a teenager, anyway, though hardly a wayward one.

Pause again. Had Emily loved the spoilt younger sister who had got away, studied and worked and lived just as she chose, leaving the elder trapped in that dismal house doing her duty? Surely she must have done in her way, or she would never have agreed to take charge of Rose's child. Or had she been directed, as so often in her life, by the dread of what the neighbours would think?

The more you thought, the more questions there were: about Emily; about Rose herself; about everything. Well, it was too late to ask Rose anything, and it was impossible to imagine questioning Emily. She would just have to start using her imagination – if she still had one after all the years of doing and thinking as she was told. Best to start small.

By the time the grass was growing chilly and the water starting to ripple under the evening breeze, she had managed quite a complete biography.

My mother's death must have been a double shock for her – not only losing her sister, but suddenly finding herself stuck with the grizzling toddler she'd agreed to look after for a weekend ... She was almost fifty and lived a very quiet, ordered life – a real spinster of the old school – and now it was all shattered by the arrival of an alien being. In fact, another alien being: Emily was many years older than my mother, the sister she never expected to have, and I know she had to help a lot with looking after her, and resented it. So how could she help resenting me?

Besides which, my aunt really doesn't care for children. They make noises, they don't keep still and they mess up the furniture. So all credit to her then, that she didn't park me in the nearest orphanage and run for her life. Instead she basically gave me the same upbringing she had herself, never thinking that times might have changed somewhat. As a result I learned not only to cook but to embroider (though I'm still waiting to find out what that's for), to sit quietly in the corner while the grown-ups talked and not to play with dirty boys. And come to think of it, that's about all I've learned to this day. Which is why, a couple of months ago, I decided to set out and see a little bit of the planet for myself. And so far it feels as if my life began on the day I made that decision.

Like that first sentence, it all seemed to have been written by someone else. This wasn't her voice. Did she even have a voice? Perhaps it was Ghislaine's. Perhaps if she thought of her new self, her writing self, as Ghislaine, a person nobody had ever met, it would be easier to say whatever she liked.

Gillian thought that when it was time to leave the Loire Valley she would travel southwards, zigzagging across the country as the weather and her whims dictated, but with the general aim of reaching the south coast. She felt drawn to Agde rather than the more famous eastern places like St Tropez or even Marseilles – Agde would surely be less crowded and, from what she could make out, cheaper. Besides, she fancied seeing a place she'd once seen described as the black pearl of the Mediterranean. And after that she supposed it would be time to start heading for home …

And here her thoughts always came to a stop. There was always so much to do: wrestling with the Trafic; the low-level repetitive tasks that go with life on a campsite; the excitement of new places; the struggle with French, which in a way grew harder as she became more ambitious in her speech; the writing, which was gradually becoming the focus of each day. It was so easy not to think beyond the next day or even the next hour. She was still preoccupied with the sensations and ideas assailing her in this new life; sometimes, when she was doing something as simple as sitting under the awning looking across at the river, or wandering around the stalls of a market-day morning, she would have to stop and tell herself: yes, this is me, Gillian, Ghislaine, I'm here, in France, on my own with nobody telling me what to do – and the terror and sweetness of the thought would leave her dizzy. She wanted only to go on with this aimless life, for a while at least, until this frail, nascent self grew strong enough to start facing the real world.

The Real World. That was the world Kate talked about in her increasingly disapproving emails. Even Aunt Emily, despite living her own life in a sort of perpetual Agatha Christie-era teatime, was perfectly sure that the Real World was where her niece belonged, and had tried her best to prepare her for it. The Real World was a place where impractical people with a yen for stories went to study administration and open savings accounts, and forget their silly ideas about writing for a living. It was where you learned the value of money and security and the uselessness of everything else. The Real World – suddenly she was half choking with pent-up resentment – was the place where a frumpy, timorous nonentity called Gillian Bailie eked out a dismal half-life chained to a formica desk in an airless building, and never once questioned what she was doing there, what any of it was for.

Evening was moving softly along the river, turning it to a dark olive green. In warm weather like this there might be bats, the huge dark monsters she had seen swooping over the quiet water; one night they had come so close, she could have sworn she saw their teeth gleaming. She sat still and felt the night settling around her shoulders, and thought: this is the real world. Not the Loire itself, though she had loved the region on sight; not even France, though she loved that too as far as she knew it. But this peace, this unutterable luxury of having time and space and freedom.

But, but. Kate and Aunt Emily weren't wrong either. As she'd heard Emily say so many times, 'Who's going to pay for it?' This luxury was hers because Auntie lived like a mouse in the shadow of her beloved church, managing on odds and ends, barely touching her small capital and never leaving her too-large childhood home; and because she herself had always lived in the same way, always saving, always buying the cheapest or going without. So who was she to feel cheated because she had been constrained by thrift and caution? They were serving her pretty well now.

Still, her savings wouldn't last forever. Sooner or later she would have to start earning, and even, one day, to think about getting a mortgage, finding a place to live. Before, it had been the responsibility of home ownership that had terrified her, and the dread of having to contend with lending rates and then HIPS and all the other mysteries that everyone else seemed to be born understanding. Now all this seemed much less daunting; it was the thought of going back to the old routine that appalled her. 'What shall I do?' said Gillian aloud, as she reluctantly went inside and pulled the little curtains on the sweet, secret blackness outside. How strange to think that, not long ago, she had been afraid of the dark.

At any rate, she thought sleepily as she assembled the bed a little later, she wouldn't go back to her old job – not that they'd want her. There must be something else she could do … no need to worry about it just yet. She would come up with something.

She spent the next two weeks meandering along the same little stretch of the great river and its tributaries. She saw Chenonceau and the Sleeping Beauty's castle at Uzay; she walked so far that she got blisters even in her invariably sensible shoes. She learned that wherever you are in the Loire region, there is always one day when all the shops are closed and the unwary visitor will go hungry. She chatted with fellow campers and shopkeepers and anyone who had time. It might be that the effort of thinking in a new language left no room for self-consciousness, or it might be because there was nobody here that she knew, nobody in whose eyes she was already established as a failure, but she was finding it easier to talk, to start a conversation, than she had ever done in her life.

One morning in early June, in the municipal campsite at Azay-le-Rideau, she woke up with a new idea: she would take a bus, pick a destination at random, get off there and write a story about whatever happened that day. Importantly packing pen and notebook into her shoulder bag, she set off for the bus stop.

The destination, Les Châtres, was a place she knew nothing about. The ride took about half an hour through white-stone villages and quiet roads bordered with fields. She kept her notebook dutifully to hand, but couldn't immediately see anything likely to make a story from. Then they were back on the river, crossing a wide suspension bridge.

For a while after getting off the bus she just wandered in the shadow of the chateau, awe-inspiring even by the standards of the Loire Valley, through the cobbled streets that flowed beneath its massive walls. Clearly as a first-time visitor she should be paying to go inside it, but the day was too perfect and the town too enticing. She slipped through the strollers and shoppers, idling in no special direction, found herself slowly moving away from the centre and the river, and presently came to a quiet residential street. Here the houses were large and the front gardens shady; she had reached the end, not only of the road but of the town itself when she noticed that the last, largest house before the fields began again had a dingy sign over the open door. Les Saules: CAFÉ BISTRO CHAMBRES D'HOTES. Gillian was thirsty and, now she thought of it, hungry. Looking again she saw a second notice, tacked on to the right of the house by hand: JARDIN, with an arrow pointing to the end wall. She pushed open the gate – it felt as if this didn't happen to it very often – and walked up the weedy path.

Inside, as far as she could see in the sudden gloom, were a bar and some tables and chairs, none of them very inviting. But through the rear door she got a glimpse of trees and a hint of breeze, and when a bored-looking man appeared from behind the door she ordered an omelette and an orange juice, and asked to have them in the garden. He made no reply but gave a small shrug, which she interpreted as a yes.

Outside she found she was the only guest; indeed apart from her surly host she seemed to be the only person around at all. She wondered about the *Chambres d'hôtes* sign, for she had seen nothing like a reception desk. She sat down at a peeling wrought-iron table and hoped the green marks on the chair didn't come off.

The garden was big, a good quarter acre, though beyond the half-dozen tables shaded by lime trees it seemed to be just long grass, and beyond that a solitary willow. Didn't *les saules* mean 'the willows'? Maybe there used to be more of them. She could see a shed close to the high stone wall at the far end and wondered what was kept in it. The whole place was rather mysterious – perhaps it belonged to a grand old family that had declined and were now reluctantly dirtying their hands in the hospitality trade. Not that she'd been offered much hospitality so far, and there was nothing grand about the house either. Never mind, it was all part of the day's adventures. As there was still no sign of the omelette she took out her notebook and began writing: *On the outskirts of*

Just then, from inside the house she heard an unmistakably Anglo-Saxon voice say, 'Why can't you cook it? You're supposed to be the one who can cook, you're happy enough sitting on your arse talking about how useless the English are—'

'So you are not able to make an omelette?' came a man's voice in coldly perfect English. 'Why am I not surprised?' The reply was inaudible, try as Gillian would to catch it. Fascinated, she started to write down the lines of dialogue, and grew so absorbed that she failed to notice that someone had come out of the house and was reading over her shoulder until a loud, angry 'Can I help you?' made her leap from her seat. It was the Englishwoman who had just been shouting in the kitchen, and she was looking down at her own words on Gillian's jotter.

'Are you some sort of journalist?' she asked.

'No, no, I'm so sorry, I just ...' Gillian half rose and sat down again. 'I just do a bit of writing now and then, and I was trying to describe this place, it's so, er, the garden is so lovely, and then I got carried away ...' She realised that she was gabbling, and the woman wasn't even listening. 'Oh, what does it matter,' she muttered, and visibly pulling herself together, dug a pad out of her grubby overall pocket. 'Anyway, about your order, I'm sorry but there's a problem.'

Gillian knew she was supposed to help her pretend nothing had happened, and then flee at the first opportunity. But instead she found herself saying, 'Yes. There is a problem, isn't there? Listen, I'm on holiday, I've got nothing to do today and I feel bad about eavesdropping on you like that. Won't you let me see if I can help?'

The woman stared a moment, started to speak, looked furtively back at the house and again at Gillian, who pulled out the other chair. Finally, with a long sigh, she sat down. She was younger than she'd seemed at first glance, no more than twenty-five, just short of plumpness with short thick brown hair and a round, pretty, slightly vacant face.

'He's gone off in a strop again – anyway I don't care what he says any more,' she said half to herself. Gillian made a small, encouraging noise. By now she was very thirsty indeed, but it would clearly be heartless to send her new friend off to fetch drinks before begging her to unburden herself. Luckily, after sitting in gloomy silence for a moment, she seemed to revive, said, 'Tell you what, if you really do have time I'll get us a drink – nobody comes in at this time anyway,' and soon the two of them were sitting under the lime tree with a carafe of white wine, a basket of bread and a jug of water.

The girl's name was Beth and the other voice Gillian had heard belonged to her husband, Luc. The business belonged to Luc's family.

'This restaurant?'

'If you call it that. It's more a café really, the real business is the guests – the *pension* – but they're always trying to take on too much. It was Luc's dad's house – I think they used to have a lot of farmland or something – and he died years ago, before we met. Amèlie, that's his mum, wouldn't sell the place – they've always lived here, family home, blah blah blah.' She sighed and took another draught of wine. 'Well, so Luc won't try and get her to sell the place or let it or anything, even though he doesn't really want to be here either. But it's not working. They're too tight to employ proper staff and they just keep muddling on, getting whoever they can to help out. And Luc seems to think I ought to help Amèlie, and she's off today and I *can't*, I can't – I can't cook at all really, and anyway I've got Hugo to look after—'

'Hugo?'

'Our little boy, he's only four. Amèlie's taken him to see her sister today, but I can't have him hanging round the kitchen all the time, can I?' Gillian murmured that of course she couldn't. She wondered how this unlikely couple had met, but decided not to ask yet. 'What', she asked, 'about Luc then? What does he do?'

'Oh well, he's been trained and he does know what he's doing, I suppose, but he doesn't care all that much – I mean, he doesn't want to let his mum down and I know he didn't use to like the idea of selling it because of the whole tradition thing, but I don't think he cares about the place that much any more. And there's only him – well, he does have a brother but he's no use at anything from what I can make out ... And I am trying to help but I know they think I'm useless. Sometimes I feel like just leaving them to it and going home but when I think of starting all over again ... I'm so tired ...'

Gillian looked round at the silent garden. The white-painted tables were dirty and the grass was long. There were bits of leaf on chairs and tables and weeds pushing through the path. And yet, 'It's a lovely garden,' she said again, and meant it.

'Too much work,' muttered Beth into the dregs of her wine. 'Oh well, time to get on. Listen, you've been—'

'Get on with what?' Gillian interrupted.

'The dinners, I guess – at least the restaurant shouldn't be busy this evening, but you can't be sure, and there are still six guests here and Amèlie won't be back in time – Luc was supposed to be doing it. And there's always god knows what to get on with – the cleaning, the gardens, the maintenance, it never stops—' She half pushed herself up with her hands and slumped down again.

'Beth,' said Gillian, 'let me help you.'

Beth looked at her with sudden suspicion. 'Is this about that article of yours?'

'Oh, come on, you know it isn't. Let me help you with the dinner.'

Beth smiled for the first time and said, 'If you're sure you mean it, I don't care if you do write the article.'

It was after eleven when Gillian got home, having only just caught the last bus. The site was silent with hardly a light showing. Not quite sober, she hit her knee against the door and almost fell through it. Once inside she realised how tired she was, but she still stayed up for a while, thinking over the day.

The kitchen was less forbidding than she would have expected; it was the kitchen of a family home, albeit a large one, rather than of a restaurant. If anyone else had been there she would have been nervous, but since Beth visibly had less idea what to do than she did herself, it was hard to see how she could make matters worse. They looked at the menu and worked out that they would need to prepare a chicken and some lamb chops first; the rest could be done later.

They chopped and scraped and seasoned with a good deal of consultation and, after a while, some giggling. They hadn't drunk any more, but there was a slightly partyish mood nonetheless. When the chicken and the vegetables were prepared they turned to dessert: tarte aux pommes or crème caramel.

'Amèlie made the caramel thing before she left today,' said Beth, 'and Luc brought back a big bag of apples yesterday – I know that, because she was moaning about them being out of season or imported or something, but he got them cheap so ... but what's the difference between a tarte aux pommes and an apple tart?'

'Well, I have had some French ones,' said Gillian, 'but I can't remember what kind of pastry they had. Just dessert pastry, I suppose. The guests must know you're English; why don't I make an English apple pie and you can tell them it's your old family recipe?'

'*Can* you make one?' Beth looked at her as if she'd said she could butcher a bull.

'Oh yes. It's even an old family recipe – my Aunt Emily's. I'll make a big one and we can cut it into slices. Just leave it to me.'

She was mixing the dough for the pastry when the dark, thin, morose figure who had taken her lunch order appeared in the doorway and the voice Gillian had heard earlier said, 'Beth, *je ne peux pas*—' Then seeing Gillian working at the other end of the big room, he strode in and demanded an explanation.

'Luc, this is Gillian; Gillian, this is my husband, Luc.' Beth sounded slightly defiant. Gillian tried to pull the sticky dough off her hands and greet Luc, who now looked even more annoyed.

'*Bonjour*, er ...'

'So you are English?' he asked, managing to make the question sound insulting. Gillian admitted that she was, left the explanations to Beth and turned back to her pastry.

Beth explained that Gillian was the guest who should have had the omelette at lunch; that she had noticed her, Beth, looking tired and offered to help.

'So now we ask the guests to come and cook their own meals? We're self-service now?' Gillian had already noticed that Luc spoke English whenever he felt like being sarcastic. She also saw that Beth, who had been quite cheerful a moment earlier, was looking as sullen and dejected as she had done when they met. She cleaned her hands on the apron she had found and turned round.

'Beth didn't ask me to do anything,' she said, hoping that her French was at least clear, 'and she didn't complain either. I could see she was exhausted, and as I have nothing to do today I insisted on helping. Now that you're back I'm sure everything will be fine, but shall I finish making this dessert, since I've started it?'

Luc looked rather taken aback and mumbled that it was very kind of her, but there was no need … Taking this for agreement she put her hands back in the mixing bowl, and Beth picked up her knife again and carried on mangling the onions. Luc stood for a while looking around, and then went out.

Beth and Gillian worked on together until late in the afternoon. They had almost finished and were just agreeing that a cup of something would be nice when there was a shriek of 'Maman!' and a small boy hurtled into the kitchen clasping a huge plastic brontosaurus. Beth tried to pick them both up at once, overbalanced and they all collapsed on the nearest chair. She shushed the little boy, who was chattering excitedly in Franglais and waving his new toy, and turned to Gillian saying, 'This is my son, Hugo. Say hello in English, Hugo.'

'Hello Hugo, my name is Gillian. What a lovely dinosaur, will you show him to me?'

The boy, who had his mother's thatch of brown hair, looked at her from under it with his father's scowl; but when Beth urged him forward he came to Gillian and, when she showed a proper interest in the dinosaur, disclosed that its name was Theo and it ate grass. He was showing her how high Theo could jump when a small, spare woman in her sixties came in, already talking before she reached the door.

'Luc, Beth, *est-ce que vous avez—*' She stopped when she saw Gillian.

Beth hurried to introduce her, explaining her away much as she had to Luc, but noticeably with a good deal more stammering. Gillian herself, who hadn't found Luc at all alarming, recognised in his mother a much stronger character. She heard her daughter-in-law out in silence and then, turning to the visitor with a cool smile, said, 'Madame, this is very kind. You must let us offer you some refreshments before you leave.'

Her boldness collapsing, Gillian accepted the offer of a cup of coffee 'in our beautiful garden', surrendered the apron and was allowing herself to be gently steered towards the door when Mme Martin, glancing round to see what damage the intruder had done, caught sight of her finished dessert sitting on the table ready for the oven and shrieked, 'What is THAT?'

'An "apple pee", Maman,' said Luc with disdain, 'I believe that's what the English call a tarte aux pommes.'

'So kind,' snapped Mme Martin, and flung the door wide. Feeling rather indignant on Emily's behalf Gillian paused and said, 'It's my aunt's recipe, and it's won prizes in her church fetes. I think your guests will enjoy it.'

'Actually, Amèlie,' said Beth, 'you know the old lady in Room 2?'

'Mme Marca?' Amèlie's voice was growing colder by the second.

'Yes, her. Well, she was asking me the other day about English food, and whether it was as bad as people here think. I said it wasn't, and she said it would be nice to try something.'

Whether or not this was true, it seemed the pie was about to be reprieved. Amèlie looked narrowly at Gillian and then asked, 'Would you tell me how long it needs to be baked?'

The ice broken, it wasn't too hard to persuade her to let Gillian help with some of the last-minute prep when Beth had to take Hugo away for bath and bed and Luc had slouched off to look after some hypothetical customers. In fact when Amèlie saw how much the two of them had achieved that afternoon, she eyed Gillian in a much friendlier manner as they added seasoning and heated plates.

'I didn't like to leave Beth in charge,' she confided; 'I know cooking isn't her forte, but Luc should have been helping her. Well, we will have to think about getting more help, but it's very hard to find anyone suitable – and then the expense. Ah well, girls today … *You* seem to know something about cooking.'

'My aunt gave me a very traditional education – to be honest, I didn't like most of it. I do like cooking, though. But I wouldn't know what to do if you were busy here – when does it get busy, Mme Martin?'

'Amèlie.' She sighed. 'It's never very busy now. Everybody talks about advertising and the internet – in my day the same families came back year after year …'

'Do you have a website?'

Another sigh. 'We have a listing in French, but we should be getting more English visitors too – they seem to love the Loire. We do need some advertising in English – yes, we should have a website, but Beth – ah well, never mind.' When Gillian looked enquiring, she said, 'That is not her forte either.'

Gillian would have felt sorry for Beth, crushed under the weight of Amèlie's weary competence, but she had just had an idea. She finished cutting up the chives before saying, very diffidently, 'In my last job I looked after the company website. If you would like me to have a look?' But she could see that by inviting herself into the secrets of the business she had gone too far. 'It was just an idea, never mind.'

'You are very kind,' said Amèlie.

When they finished serving dinner Amèlie invited Gillian to stay, but she wouldn't add to their work. 'Then,' said Amèlie, 'you must visit us again – as our guest this time.' With no idea whether she meant it, Gillian accepted.

Very sleepy now, she stretched out on the narrow bed and closed her eyes. Her legs ached and she'd been working for hours without a break, but she had just had one of the best days of her life. And how sad is that? was her last thought before she drifted away.

10: Work

The next day Gillian was restless and, for the first time in weeks, low-spirited. She wanted to go back to Les Saules, but she couldn't face turning up there so soon and being greeted by Amèlie with chilly courtesy, ushered to a table at a safe distance from all the action and perhaps forced to sit and consume a complimentary lunch that would choke her with embarrassment. No, she would have to accept the day for what it was – a lively interlude and material for a piece of writing.

A piece of writing. That was an idea. After all, although she might drop in once more before she left the region, effectively she and the Martin family would never meet again, and in the unlikely event that she found a publisher why would any of them read anything she might write? The weather was turning steadily warmer; she would pull a big towel from under the banquette, spread it out near the river bank and settle down with her notebook and pencil as she had done when she first started writing – the laptop felt too official today.

By evening she was almost done and had hardly stirred from her waterside spot. She had never written anything so quickly. Reading it over, it struck her that she had been slightly unfair – Amèlie a cartoon *belle-mère* with starched apron and pursed lips, Beth a feeble *anglaise*, unable to peel a potato and weeping at the threat of hard work, and Luc all glowering eyebrows and sudden, theatrical exits and entrances. It was worrying how easily it had all come to her.

She typed it out and emailed it to all the addresses she had found earlier – camping magazines, women's magazines, expat websites – and decided to visit the house again next day. She would say goodbye and then move on and find something else to write about; and if she didn't get anything accepted by the end of the summer, well, she would worry about that at the end of the summer.

She arrived in Les Châtres about eleven the next morning and went straight to Les Saules. She guessed it would be best just to have a coffee, chat to Beth for a few minutes and then be off before the lunchtime rush – if they ever had one – started. She pushed her way through the stiff gate again and went into the bar, but this time no Luc came muttering out of the dark. She went through to the garden and found that empty too.

She hovered for a while in the garden doorway, trying to catch a sound, but the place might have been the *Marie Celeste.* She was about to leave when she heard a small bewildered voice saying 'Maman?' and Hugo came out into the bar, clutching the dinosaur he'd brought back from his great-aunt's. He looked furtive when he saw her – she guessed he wasn't allowed in here – but when she greeted him in French he forgot about that.

'You're Mummy's friend,' he told her, in a loftily correct English that reminded her of Luc. 'You're English. I speak English very well.'

'Yes, you do, Hugo,' she placated him. 'And can you find Mummy for me?'

But just then a door cracked open and Beth came rushing out, crying, 'Hugo! Hugo, where—' and seeing Gillian, stopped dead. 'Oh,' she said after a moment, 'hello, er, Gillian. Sorry, I wasn't expecting to—'

Gillian said soothingly, 'Hello, Beth, it's all right, Hugo's fine. He only looked in here to see who it was, he wasn't going outside—' But although Beth had almost automatically taken him by the shoulders and pulled him protectively close, it was clear that something else was worrying her. 'Gillian,' she said, 'we're ever so grateful for the other night and of course you're welcome here any time, but just now …'

Gillian was desperately embarrassed. 'I haven't come for free cakes, Beth! I just came to say, well, goodbye really, because I'm probably moving on tomorrow, but of course you're busy! I'll get out of your way—' She was backing towards the door as she spoke. Then Beth burst out, 'It's not that, Amèlie's ill and I haven't got a clue what to do!'

She sounded slightly hysterical, worse than she had seemed the other day. Surely the whole house didn't collapse just because Amèlie was ill? But it seemed Luc had had to go and get a delivery, new guests were coming and nothing was done.

'So where is Amèlie now?'

'She had to go back to bed. She won't have a doctor, she just gets these migraines and she always says she'll be fine tomorrow. So I've sorted out the room for the new people, but now there's another couple leaving in about an hour, and I haven't a clue how you do the bills or anything. And then if anyone comes in for lunch ...' She was growing tearful.

'Well, nobody did the other day except me,' said Gillian, thinking how easy it was to be brisk about other people's problems, 'and if they do we'll tell them everything's off except omelettes, and I can make those. So shall we have a look at the bill? I mean,' she added quickly as Beth hesitated, 'if you'll let me? Amèlie needn't know, need she?'

Beth turned to Hugo, who had climbed onto a bar stool by this time and was pouring imaginary drinks for Theo. 'Hugo,' she said, 'I want you to go upstairs to Grandmère and ask her if she needs anything. Off you go, there's a good boy.'

They went into the dark interior of the old house and Beth led the way into a narrow room off the hall. It was full of papers and folders, all neatly filed and labelled. It was easy to see that this was Amèlie's stronghold and not

Beth's. The room had an old-fashioned air – it could almost have been an office in a black and white film, except for an ancient monitor grudgingly given room at one end of a desk.

'I don't really care if Hugo tells Amèlie you were in here,' Beth said, 'I had to do something, didn't I? but I just wanted to explain – she doesn't like computers. Luc made her a database but she hates using it, and now everything's in a real mess. And I don't know anything about admin either.' She tapped a key and the screen brightened to reveal a spreadsheet.

After a few minutes Gillian was relieved to see that the system wasn't too hard to use. The only problem was that Amèlie, mistrusting the strange new technology, hadn't entered a lot of the information in the fields Luc had set up for her. But it didn't take long to find the details in her old-fashioned ledger. By the time Hugo came back saying that Grandmère was asleep, the two of them had almost finished the bill.

'You make everything seem so easy,' Beth said later, when they were gulping a quick coffee before it was time to start the dinners. 'Have you worked in a place like this before?'

'No! I don't really know anything, it's just …' Just that when you've gone all your life thinking you couldn't do the simplest thing, when you finally try you can't get over how easy it is, this living business. 'It's just that you need another person here, don't you? There's too much for you and Amèlie to do – and Luc.'

'Luc,' said Beth bitterly. Gillian waited for more, but Beth seemed to be lost in thought. Only when they were mixing the salads did she say, 'Of course we need another person. I wish you weren't going tomorrow.'

Gillian had been thinking too. Now she said, 'I don't have to go. I was only moving on because I thought I'd like to see a bit more of the country; I really haven't got any plans. Beth, if I stayed a bit longer couldn't I help out here? I like this place so much, and I was going to have to look for work soon anyway.'

'But don't you have a job? I thought you were a writer or something.'

Gillian sighed. 'If only I was. I used to work in an accountancy firm. I left because I wanted to do some travelling, but of course I'll have to find another job soon. But I want to stay in France for the summer at least – do you think we could work something out?'

11: Summer

The little plot of land was probably too small to be called a field, but that seemed the easiest way to explain it to Kate.

I've got a summer job! I'm helping out in a little café/restaurant/B&B not far from Tours, and have moved my van into a tiny field at the back. Since there's nothing there except me and a couple of fruit trees, it feels almost like having my own place. And I can hook up to the mains in the house, so I get electricity and everything laid on. I can have showers there – there is one in the van but it isn't much good. And I get most of my meals – in fact I'm being fed like a prize pig – so even though they're really only paying me pocket money, I have no expenses and I think it's worth staying through the summer season at least. After that

She stared for a while at the screen and then deleted the last two words. No need to attract any more lectures from Kate or Aunt Emily about the future. There would be enough of those when they realised she wasn't coming back until the end of August at the earliest.

I'm just going to call Auntie E and tell her. She won't like it but it's doing me the world of good and my French is coming on so well! I'll be able to put that on my CV all right when I get back.

True as far as it went, and it might satisfy Aunt Emily if she could tell the church ladies 'Gillian is staying on for a while to improve her French', but as good as it felt to find herself understanding a little more every week, that wasn't what was keeping her here. The sense of freedom, of every day being a new adventure, was increased, not lessened, now that she was working. This wasn't like working at Evans', toiling in the dark like an ant and never daring to ask what it was all for. At Les Saules there seemed to be a minor emergency almost every day, and helping to keep things going felt like real work with a purpose – even if the purpose was no more than feeding and housing a succession of guests and keeping them from complaining.

It hadn't been easy to persuade Amèlie. But she was still weak from her latest migraine and Luc had been so relieved at coming home and finding most of the work done that he gave his grudging support. He was still barely polite; it was clear that he believed his wife ought to be able to do the work that Gillian was now doing, and that he strongly – and correctly – suspected that Beth spent a lot of time complaining about him to her new British ally. Still, Gillian's presence was making his own life easier and they tolerated each other.

The success of the apple pee notwithstanding, she had none of the skills of a professional chef and the best she could do was act as an occasional helper to Amèlie. But she was learning, just as she was learning how to get a room ready for a new occupant at lightning speed and deal with the arcane billing system. And for the first time in her life she was neither a burden nor invisible. Amèlie snapped at her sometimes when she was slow or dropped things, but she also devoted time to teaching her, and once unguardedly remarked that she might have been unfair in judging 'English girls'. She took it back at once – she never openly criticised Beth, who was now family – but Gillian understood her well enough.

As part of her payment she was regularly invited to take meals with the family, usually in the early afternoon when there was nothing to do for the guests. As delicious as Amèlie's cooking was, and Luc's too when he could be bothered, she took care not to accept every day. Partly she was afraid of becoming a nuisance, partly of losing her independence, and she had arranged things so that nobody was surprised if she said she had work to do or was going on an excursion for the afternoon. Besides, she still wasn't used to spending time with groups of people and they weren't the most comfortable of dining companions. Meals were almost the only time that the whole family sat together, and the tensions between Luc and Beth, and Beth and Amèlie – and even between Amèlie and her son – were plain to see. Amèlie and Luc would rebuke Hugo for bad table manners or noise and Beth would leap to his defence; or an apparently innocent remark about a job needing to be done would cause Beth or Luc to protest that they were doing all they could and had no more time.

It didn't take long to find out how Beth had ended up here. Only a few days into her stay, seeing how Les Saules was struggling to keep going Gillian started comparing its prices with those of other places nearby, and remarked to Beth that the Martins seemed to be charging less than most.

Beth sighed. 'Yes, they're cheap all right. Well, that's why we came in the first place – I mean, I came with my mum and dad. It was meant to be a treat after I finished college. This friend of theirs had a house in Chinon and we were going to stay there, but then at the last minute she let us down – she let it to someone, and it was the only time we could go so we just asked if she knew of anywhere else. She came up with this place and they had rooms free – well, they always do, I know that now.'

'So that's how you and Luc met?'

'Yes.' She sighed again. 'Mum and Dad loved it here but I was bored out of my mind. And so I started going out with Luc sometimes instead of going off with them to see chateau after chateau. He's quite a bit older than me, I thought he was the coolest ... ' She trailed off and looked out of the window.

'And you stayed here?' Gillian reflected that she was getting quite clever at encouraging people to talk. Maybe she could be a proper journalist one day.

Not that getting Beth to talk needed much skill. She told the rest of her story in a rush; she had gone home with her parents and she and Luc had kept up a fitful relationship. Although she didn't say as much, it sounded as if it would have faded away soon enough; but then Hugo had changed everything.

'I didn't really know what I was going to do. I told Mum and she said I'd better tell Luc and ... They were really good, I'll give them that. Amèlie just seemed to take it for granted that I'd be having the baby and living with them, and Luc and I would be getting married, and ... Oh, I didn't know what I wanted if I'm honest, and I was quite scared and it just seemed so easy to let her organise everything. And Luc was over the moon when we found it was going to be a boy. Not that that lasted long.'

To Gillian it sounded like a perfectly dreadful start to a marriage, but what did she know of human relations? Maybe this was just the way people lived their lives in the Real World. There was no doubt, though, that Beth was unhappy now. She'd even gone back to her parents, briefly, when Hugo was about a year old.

'So then what happened? Did Luc come after you?' It was hard to imagine.

'No, I came back here in the end. It was just so difficult at home ...'

When the two of them were alone she complained, more and more openly, about the house, the work that seemed to be expected of her, Luc's unfairness and the general awfulness of the French, which ranged from not smiling in shops to pronouncing her name as Bet. Gillian realised that, as a fellow expat, she was supposed to agree with it all, but she avoided taking sides. Of course, to find yourself uneasily married, isolated in a country you would never have chosen to live in, doing work you disliked and with a mother-in-law who at best tolerated you, must be a dismal fate; and as much as she herself liked and respected Amèlie, she could certainly be intimidating if you fell short of her standards. Intimidating to anyone who hadn't grown up with Aunt Emily, at any rate. On the other hand, she did wonder if Beth could have made things easier for herself. 'Of course it's easy for you,' she said to Gillian once, 'you speak really good French.' Gillian didn't point out that she spoke French because she had taken the trouble to learn it, or that Beth had had nearly five years to do the same. She could communicate and mainly understand, but it was clear that she had no intention of learning any more. She and Luc spoke English with Hugo, and Luc had grown a good deal more fluent in English than she had in French. As with the language, so with the work. Hugo took most of her free time, to be sure; but although he was at the École Maternelle for several hours a day now, she did only what couldn't be avoided and was interested in none of it.

But just as well for me she isn't interested, thought Gillian. I'm not doing anything that she couldn't.

A lot of the pleasure was novelty, she knew that. Here was another, larger doll's house to make a change from the tiny Trafic. And she had little to do with the heavier work, the washing and ironing, the gardening and the more complicated cooking. But when she finally gained permission to start on the English-language website she wasn't playing. She laboured over it, took pictures of the house from inside and out and even wheedled a stiff camera-smile out of Amèlie. And once the bookings from Britain started to come in, Amèlie began to treat Gillian almost with affection. She only hoped that when the rosbifs arrived they would behave themselves.

Anyway, it's a lovely spot, and now they're sorting out the garden it would be a perfect place for a holiday. I showed you the new website, didn't I? You know, you should think about bringing Al and the kids here for a break.

I only work part-time and there would be plenty of time to show you around. They don't ask me to do very much at all – a lot of things I volunteer for, like going to the bakery in the mornings and looking after the website. So I've got lots of time to try a bit of writing – can't get wifi in the van of course, but Amèlie lets me use the little back office as much as I want. So I can check my emails every day, but I'm sending all my contacts this postal address as well, just in case.

She saved the draft, closed the laptop and went off to count the towels for the laundry, wondering what Kate would say when she read the email. 'Look at this, Al – poor Gill, she's obviously run out of money and now she's working for pocket money in some French B & B. God help them if she's all the help they can get.' And Al would mumble, 'Well, she sounds happy,' and Kate would laugh shortly and say, 'Well, she's got to put a good face on it, hasn't she? She knows we all thought it was a mad idea to go. I give it three weeks.'

She found all kinds of jobs to do that day, even after Amèlie had said, 'There is nothing important, go and enjoy yourself.' She knew perfectly well why she was being so diligent: anything at all to delay making the call to Emily. Just as she had imagined Kate reading the email, it was all too easy to hear the conversation with her aunt: 'So you're a chambermaid? Or do you mean a waitress? I see. And how long are you planning to stay there? … living in your caravan, I see. So you won't be coming home this summer? No, no, I shall be perfectly all right. It's yourself you should be worrying about.'

When the evening came there was no way of putting it off any longer. She asked to use the office landline, insisting on paying – she had never bought a new mobile, for there seemed no use for it at present. She waited until Beth had gone to put Hugo to bed and Luc was in the bar, feeling embarrassed at being overheard placating her aunt, thrown back to her old spiritless self.

In fact Aunt Emily was rather odd in her manner. She seemed off-hand if anything, and had little to say about her niece's new career beyond 'Oh yes? That will keep you busy.'

Gillian persisted, 'And you, Aunt Emily? How are you getting on with Jenny, is she a help?'

'Jenny who? Oh yes, Jenny. No, I haven't needed her to come yet. I'm managing very well.'

'Are you? Well, of course that's wonderful, but you will ask her to come if you need any help, won't you?'

After Gillian had rung off she felt a little piqued – disapproval was more natural than indifference, surely. But after all, if Aunt Emily was too busy with her own concerns to censure anyone else, that was surely a good thing. She must remember to ask Kate if she knew what might be keeping Emily so preoccupied.

In the second week of July the weather turned much hotter and grew sticky, making the gentle Loire climate feel more like southern England in a heatwave. The guests and the people she met around the town ambled about their business; Amèlie grew paler and her mouth closed tighter as the sultry weather made her headaches worse; but Gillian, now permanently in shorts or thin cotton trousers, found that the weather hardly troubled her. She got up early and did most of her work before noon, dozed for a while in the afternoon, sat under the awning and wrote or strolled by the river or climbed the hills above the town in the evening, and on her free days took the bus and went exploring. Only the van was sometimes too hot at night; but she kept all the windows open and the screens up against mosquitoes, and if sleep wouldn't come lay and listened to the distant water and the faint sighing of the willows.

As the summer days passed she began to wonder how much longer she could stay here. Once high season was over Amèlie would surely have no reason to let her stay on

– she might not actually be in the way, but in quieter times she surely wouldn't be of much use either. But what if she could find some more permanent work; if not here, then there must be something elsewhere? Could she live in the van in the winter? Could she earn enough to rent a place to stay?

One searingly hot morning in August she was in the back garden of the house, looking at the plum trees to see how much fruit there was left after Amèlie's jam-making. There seemed to be plenty more and she pulled off a yellow mirabelle and ate it slowly. It was headily sweet and dripping with juice; they'd need to use these soon. She tossed the stone into the hedge, thinking she might try and trim that a bit if there was time, and was turning towards the house when the gate creaked and a hesitant voice behind her said, '*Est-ce je peux vous aider?*'

Gillian whirled round, already feeling herself turning scarlet. The owner of the voice was a tall man, fair and slightly stooped, and he seemed as embarrassed as she was. They both began to speak at once, stopped and invited the other to continue. Gillian had got as far as 'Er, *je ...*' when Hugo came bursting through the open door and charged up to them shrieking '*Oncle Hervé, Oncle Hervé!*'

The new arrival scooped up the little boy and swung him up among the branches so that the leaves tickled him and he squealed with delight. So this was the waste-of-space brother! She had imagined a slower version of Luc, with the scowl but without the occasional bursts of energy – certainly not this shy stranger who seemed to feel less at home in the *pension* than she did.

He wasn't timid with the child, though. It was some time before they finished playing and Hugo, set back on the ground, turned to her crying, 'Gillienne, Gillienne, Oncle Hervé is here!'

'And will you introduce me to Gillienne, Hugo?' Hervé asked solemnly, at the same time giving her an apologetic half-smile. 'Gillienne, this is my uncle Hervé,' Hugo said with equal gravity. 'Oncle Hervé, Gillienne is Maman's friend. She lives in the field and she helps Grand-mère. And she's from England like Maman, but it's all right, she understands everything we say, don't you, Gillienne?'

Gillian decided it was time to explain. 'I was travelling in my, er, camping-car and your mother very kindly let me stay here. I give a bit of help when they're busy. Anyway, I must get on now, your mother is inside, er ...' It felt odd to be welcoming Amèlie's son to what was presumably his own home, but she had a strong feeling that without encouragement he might turn tail and run. Hugo seized his hand and dragged him inside, and Gillian retreated to her van. You couldn't intrude on a reunion, joyful or otherwise, though she would have given something to see how they all welcomed him. Anyway, there was unlikely to be a jam-making session today by the look of things.

She was sprawling on the grass in the shade of the apple tree, notebook in hand, pretending that she was thinking of ideas for a new article but really just lazing, when the click of the meadow gate made her sit up.

Beth came slowly forward. It had never been spelled out whether Gillian's pitch included use of the field; but except for Hugo, who regarded the van as a playroom, they all treated the little patch of grass as if it were her private garden.

Gillian smiled welcomingly and patted the space beside her. 'I was just going to make tea,' she lied, 'have you got time for one?' Sometimes Beth's visits to her pitch, which usually took place when she had something to complain about, grew a little tedious; but today Gillian was curious to hear about the visitor.

She wasn't disappointed. Beth flopped down and launched straight in with 'You won't have met Luc's brother yet.'

'Just as he was coming in,' said Gillian. 'I was a bit surprised. Didn't he tell anyone he was coming?'

Beth seemed a little annoyed at being deprived of the news, but resumed her story. 'No, and it looks like he's not even staying. He says he's staying in Tours. Amèlie's not best pleased, I know that. She was asking if his old home wasn't good enough, all that sort of thing.'

'So why isn't he staying here?'

'Well, as far as I can tell he's doing some work around here. I'm not sure what, lecturing or something' – Gillian was surprised again. What would the wastrel brother be lecturing on, and who would want to hear him? – 'and it was at short notice and he's using a friend's flat in Tours to save commuting. If you ask me he could have come to stay easily. It's not much further, is it? But he never comes near the family if he can help it.'

Gillian made tea while Beth told her what she knew about Hervé. He was older than Luc, though only by two years, and according to Luc was 'no use'. He had never shown any interest in the family business, but had gone off to university – she thought to study history, but wasn't sure – and now was some sort of lecturer. 'Evening classes I think, or whatever they have. And he lives in Orléans, so it's not far, but like I said he hardly ever shows his face here.'

'Hugo seems very fond of him.'

'Oh yes, Hugo's with him now playing some game. He's a nice enough guy really, I suppose. Not got a lot to say for himself.'

'He seemed a bit shy to me,' said Gillian.

Beth looked contemptuous. 'Yes, he wouldn't say boo to a goose and if you ask me, he's terrified of Amèlie.' So are you, thought Gillian, but she knew by now that empathy was not, as Amèlie would say, Beth's forte. For her part, she was sorry for the visitor; it was easy to imagine Amèlie's, and no doubt her late husband's exasperation at finding a son of theirs no use at the family business and not even making a success of something else.

Gillian decided to go into town and get something to eat from the Petit Casino, leaving the family to have their meal together. However, as she was setting off Amèlie came out of the house and urged her to join them. She seemed very sincere; perhaps the strain of dealing with the disappointing son was telling already?

Never very lively, the atmosphere around the table in the dark private sitting-dining room was more subdued than ever. Amèlie stalked in and out with plates and tureens, refusing all offers of help. Gillian was placed next to Hervé, who gave her another nervous half-smile and became absorbed in his plate.

After the dessert Amèlie went into the kitchen and showed no sign of coming back. After a particularly long silence Luc suddenly asked his brother, 'So you're staying in Tours for the whole month?'

Hervé nodded but said nothing. Luc resumed, 'And you're doing, what was it again?'

Hervé took a while to reply. 'I'm doing some research on Foulque Nerra for next term and I'm giving a course on the history of the chateau.'

'So you're not actually working then?' Luc was clearly trying to pick a fight; equally clearly, Hervé had no idea of defending himself. 'Well …' he managed before turning back to his wineglass.

'We are in trouble here, did you know? Maman' – he lowered his voice and glanced at the closed door – 'Maman isn't very well. We need more help.'

'Shall we talk about this tomorrow, Luc?' Hervé said with a glance in Gillian's direction.

'I would, but you'll have disappeared again, won't you? and don't mind Gillienne, she's quite one of the family, aren't you, Gillienne? My wife spends enough time gossiping with her—'

Hugo, who had been sitting in silence clutching Theo, suddenly said, 'Why are you angry, Papa?'

Luc glanced at him. 'I'm not, we're just talking.'

'But you are angry—'

'Beth,' Luc turned on his wife, 'Isn't it time your son was taught some manners? or is this the English way?' Beth looked sullen, Hugo offended. 'I'm not English,' he began shrilly.

'*Tais-toi*, Hugo,' Hervé said softly, with a wink at the boy that only Gillian saw. Hugo gave a secret giggle and turned back to Theo. The silence grew until Amèlie came back in with a tray of coffee.

Trying not to gulp hers down too obviously but anxious to leave the family to carry on with their quarrel in private, Gillian asked Amèlie, 'Would you like me to help with the books tomorrow?'

Amèlie, who was looking even more tired than usual, raised heavy eyes from her cup and said, after a pause, 'No, thank you, Gillienne, not until the next day; I have to arrange a few things first. But if you could help me upstairs for a while that would be very kind.'

'Of course; I'll come in early.' Gillian got up. 'Well, I must get back. Thank you so much, Amèlie; good night, everyone.' She escaped into the bright late afternoon, but instead of going back to her little plot she went out through the front gate towards the quiet lanes that bordered the fields, and strolled there in the shade for a while, thinking how little she knew of family life. Had she really been missing as much as she'd always believed? For the first time it crossed her mind that her own peculiar upbringing, that almost Victorian set-up of aunt and orphaned niece, might be worth writing about, not just for herself but for others to read. But how – an article, a story?

She was still so absorbed as she came back that she almost walked into a tall figure emerging from the garden; he recoiled, apologising, and she realised it was Hervé. Recognising her at the exact same moment, he stammered something she couldn't catch. As before, she took courage from his obvious nervousness.

'I was just taking a little walk before I go back,' she explained, 'my camping-car is just over there in the field.'

He looked curiously at her. 'You really do live in a camping-car?'

'Well, not all the time – only for the last few months. I wanted to spend more time in France and it seemed like the best way.'

'So this is a holiday?'

'In a way it is, yes. I love it here, I'd like to stay—' then, afraid he might think she was planning to squat in the field indefinitely, she broke off.

'Here in the Loire, you mean? or here in this house?'

'Both – I love the region and I like being here. Your mother has been so kind and I like helping in the *pension*, I don't know much but I enjoy it. It's so different from my life in England—' She realised that she was on the verge of telling her life story to a stranger, which Aunt Emily would certainly have condemned as both rude and likely to lead to all sorts of evils. 'But the region too, it's so interesting. Didn't you say you were giving a course about it?'

He reddened slightly. 'Er, yes, I do give some courses about local history. In fact, I am giving one lecture at the *cercle d'amitie anglais-francais* in Tours; do you know it? to a, I think you call it a historical society. They are visiting Tours soon and I, well, it was stupid of me to agree. The talk will be in French, but some of them don't speak French very well …' Gillian did know of the *cercle d'amitie*, or at least she had crept past the library where they met in dread that a horde of friendly expats might leap out at her. Hervé started to speak again, interrupted himself and seemed about to give up. As before, she found herself wanting to help him. 'You're giving a lecture? This summer?'

'Yes,' he managed, 'and, well, I wondered if – that is, I foolishly offered to make a summary and translate it into English, and the fact is my English isn't good—'

Before he could fade away altogether, Gillian asked, 'Do you think I could possibly help?' and then felt a fool; of course that wasn't what he'd meant.

Apparently it was. Even though he was still failing to look her in the eye, she could see that he was delighted. 'That's very, I mean, I don't like to ask …'

'Really,' said Gillian, 'there's nothing I'd like better. I want to know more about this place anyway, and it would be good for my French. Just let me know.'

'Thank you very much,' said Hervé in a manner that was both formal and sincere. 'I will bring my notes on my next visit, then.'

'Are you coming again soon?' she asked without thinking, and felt her face grow hot. 'I mean, er, I mean, I suppose you need to have everything ready quite soon?'

'Yes, I give the lecture in two weeks. If we could have a meeting that would be very good. Can I call you?' He didn't seem embarrassed now.

'Well, I'm afraid I don't have a phone any more. I've got email, but it only works if I bring my laptop to the house. But you can always leave a message with your family, I'm in every day.'

'Yes …' He looked dubious. 'Anyway, I would certainly appreciate your help – but anyway, I must go – thank you so much.' He made an awkward grab for her hand, shook it energetically and loped off down the avenue. She drew back into the tree shadows and watched him get into a car that looked too small for him and drive off with a lurch.

Gillian went back to the Trafic, poured herself a glass of wine and sat pondering. She remembered Beth saying Hervé hadn't much to say for himself, which was odd because, for her, he was the easiest person to talk to in the whole family. She hoped he would come again, with his lecture notes – she imagined them chaotic and tentative, handwritten with much crossing out – but wondered if he would. He seemed anxious to see as little of his family as possible.

12: Hervé

Beth lost no time in coming to talk over Hervé's visit next day. 'Well, I don't suppose we'll see him again before Christmas. Did you see? as soon as Luc talked about needing help he couldn't wait to get away. No use expecting anything from him.'

'What sort of help do you want?' Gillian said. 'I mean, does he know anything about the business?'

'Well, he grew up with it, didn't he? He could do something, that's what Luc says.'

Gillian tried and failed to imagine the man she had met last night serving drinks in the bar, or chopping up mounds of vegetables, or even driving off to fetch groceries.

'Did he use to help? When they were younger?'

'Oh, Luc says he was never any good. Well, you can see he's so far up himself—'

Usually Gillian gave only the vaguest of responses to Beth's complaints, but the fraught afternoon was still vivid in her memory and she said sharply, 'It looked to me as if he was so scared of being put down that he could hardly say a word!'

Beth looked at her in surprise. 'And how long have you known him, five minutes?'

'I can see when someone's feeling awkward. Why does Luc get so angry with him? He'd only just got there after all.'

'Oh, I don't know, Luc seems to get angry about anything at all these days.' She looked more than usually discontented this morning. 'He's always on at me, or Hugo. Maybe he does pick on Hervé ... But I think, something he said ... I think Amèlie wanted Hervé to go to university, so they never made him help out as much as Luc, and then of course he never made any money or anything. And there was something else as well, something to do with the old man, but Luc won't say much about that.'

That was all Beth knew, but it was enough to make Gillian doubt that they would be seeing Hervé again any time soon. His mother's silent reproaches must be at least as hard to bear as Luc's open resentment.

But one afternoon a few days later, she looked through the back window of the Trafic and saw him fumbling at the meadow gate. She stepped out under the awning and came to meet him.

Although he must have come in search of her, he still became flustered and apologetic as soon as he caught sight of her. 'Ah, Gillienne, *bonjour*' – he shook hands hastily – 'am I disturbing you?'

She was about to start washing out her underwear, but decided not to tell him that. 'No, Hervé, not at all, I'm free this afternoon.' As he seemed unsure how to proceed, she asked gently, 'Is it about your lecture?'

'Yes! that's right, er, I have my notes here if you're quite sure that you don't mind—'

'No, I'd love to. That's if your family …' She wasn't sure what she wanted to say. Don't mind? Won't interrupt? He seemed to understand and said, 'I've just been visiting my mother. She's lying down now, and Luc and Beth have taken Hugo to town.'

Feeling foolishly relieved, as if they were about to break some rule, she said, 'Come and sit here; it's quite shady under the – what is the word, anyway?' She pointed to the awning. 'I think we call it a *tente*,' said Hervé dubiously, 'unless there is some other word. I don't know much about camping-cars.'

'Under the *tente* – thank you. Would you like some coffee?' She rather hoped he would refuse, as she had nothing but instant and was sure that wouldn't be good enough for a French visitor. To her surprise he said, 'Do you perhaps have tea?'

This was promising. Soon they were sitting at the rickety plastic table with their mugs. Hervé had brought a sheaf of notes; the bulk of the work was typed but he had scrawled all over it, and his writing was just as erratic as Gillian had pictured it. It took her a while to decipher his system of stars and arrows all over the page, but eventually she was able to make it out. The third sentence read: *This castle exists since medieval times, but people have lived there long before.*

'Um, it should be "has existed since medieval times", and "people lived there",' she said diffidently; it occurred to her that she had quite possibly never corrected anyone in her life.

Hervé looked puzzled and then laughed, losing his anxious expression for the first time since they had met. 'Of course! the same mistakes I always made at school ... perhaps sometime you would explain it to me? My teachers tried, but I never understood a word.'

'If you'll explain the French subjunctive to me,' Gillian said, and laughed too. She read on, feeling much more comfortable. Hervé's written English actually looked better than her own written French. She wondered how well he spoke it; probably also a lot better than he realised. There wasn't a great deal to change in the lecture notes, though he seemed to have trouble believing this. 'You mean it's right? all this part here?'

'It looks all right to me, anyway,' she said. She was too busy puzzling over his handwriting and looking for mistakes to get much idea of what the lecture was actually about, but it made sense.

When they had finished he shook the papers together and looked at them again. 'This is so helpful, Gillienne, thank you. You're sure that it's all right?'

'It's fine,' she promised. 'I'd say it's ready now. When did you say you were giving the talk?'

'Next week, on Friday evening.'

And then, partly because he still looked unsure, and partly for some other reason, she said, without thinking, 'Hervé, would you mind very much if I came to the lecture?'

In surprise he looked straight at her for the first time; his eyes, she saw, were a dark grey like Amèlie's. 'You want to hear it?'

'Yes, I do.'

'I should be honoured,' said Hervé, so entirely without irony that she felt herself turning red and had to jump up with offers of fresh tea. He accepted – he seemed in no hurry at all today – and she went in to make it. She had filled the saucepan from the tap and was lighting the gas when she noticed him standing awkwardly in the doorway. She smiled at him abstractedly, since the gas was apt to sputter, and said, 'Would you like to have a look at the van? It's a Renault – well, you know that.'

'No, I really know nothing about cars. But did you buy it here? You wanted to go camping in France?'

'No, not exactly. I came from England by car, you see, and then I had an accident ...' She told him the story of the Trafic, and the first days of struggling to deal with it; soon she was opening doors and pointing out the mystifying locks and switches that had caused her so much trouble in the first days. Hervé listened attentively, helping her when she stumbled over a word and asking questions too: was it difficult to drive? didn't she mind driving on the right? what about staying on the campsites alone, or even here?

Wholly unused to being drawn out or to having any sort of audience, Gillian found herself talking more than she had ever talked, sober, to anyone in her life. They had taken their tea outside and drunk it before she came to a halt and stammered an apology for chattering so much. 'Please don't apologise,' said Hervé, 'I'm interested. You know, I've never just gone off travelling like that. What did your family think about it?'

'I don't have a family except for my aunt. She thinks I've gone mad and I'll regret it, but then she's lived in the same village all her life and never done anything except bake cakes for the church.'

'And what did you do? Did you bake cakes for the church too?'

'No. Well, I helped her sometimes when I was a girl, but I don't have anything to do with the church now – never did after I left school. And I've no right to say that about Aunt Emily, because all I ever did was go to work and, well, nothing else really. And one day I woke up and thought, all right, I'm going to France! So I left my job and my poor aunt – and here I am.'

'And what next? will you stay here?'

'Ohhh,' she sighed, feeling all at once heavy and sad. 'I can't stay here forever, and, well, I honestly don't know what I should do next.' She looked up at him with a smile. 'I'm trying to avoid thinking about it. But what about you? I don't know anything about your job, and I'd like to.'

He had been sitting quite relaxed, leaning back in the silly little plastic chair as if it were perfectly comfortable, but now he almost froze, as if someone had suddenly trained a spotlight on him, and immediately became hesitant and awkward again. 'Oh, it's not interesting, you know, I teach history, that's all.'

She persisted, much as he had done with her. Was it local history he cared about most? French national history, or world history? Did he do a lot of research? Presently he relaxed again and began to give coherent answers. He was starting to describe the course he would be teaching at a college in Orléans when the gate opened and Beth came into the meadow.

She stopped dead when she saw Hervé, who leapt up and said, 'Ah, hello, Beth, I just stopped to ... so where is Hugo?' Really, thought Gillian, you would think he was married to her.

Beth didn't trouble to hide her amazement. 'Luc's taken him out in the truck – have you been here ever since you left the house, then?'

Hervé seemed to have reverted to his usual state of uneasy silence around his family, so Gillian said, 'Yes, Hervé's giving a talk in English soon and I was asking about it. I think I'd like to go and see it, would you, Beth?' And aren't I the diplomat, she thought; when did that happen?

'Well, yes,' Hervé mumbled. Beth, who seemed to have picked up Luc's manner of speaking to her brother-in-law, snapped, 'Aren't you lucky to have all that spare time? Gillian, we've got two last-minute bookings for tomorrow and Amèlie sent me to ask if you could come and help this evening.'

'Yes, of course,' Gillian got up. She turned to Hervé and said, 'Thank you so much for telling me about your lecture; I can't wait to hear it. What time is it exactly?'

'At seven in the evening on Friday – but I would, I mean,' he looked helplessly towards Beth, who was clearly waiting to escort Gillian back to the house. They both waited for him to finish. Eventually he produced, 'Perhaps I can help too if you're so busy today?'

'*You*?' Beth said. 'Well, you'd better come back with us then.' The three of them filed through the gate and up the dusty path.

Hervé was, Gillian secretly admitted, not much use in the *pension*. He was willing enough, but his long limbs were always in the way and he seemed to have no initiative at all. Amèlie sensibly gave him some names to check and parked him in the office, where he remained hidden until Luc arrived and Hugo, with shrieks of excitement, flushed his uncle from his hiding-place and dragged him into the kitchen. Not long afterwards Hervé muttered a farewell and drifted off into the early evening, promising to come back as soon as he could and responding to Luc's 'Thank god for that, how could we possibly manage without you?' with a weak smile.

He didn't come again that week. As Friday came Gillian wondered whether she should still go to the lecture. Did he really want her to go? It would be a shame if she made him even more nervous – but didn't he do this for a living? Part of his living, anyway. And she wanted to go. She was curious to see how a man who couldn't look his own relatives in the eye would stand up in front of a roomful of people and talk to them for an hour.

Besides, she liked him. He might be a disappointment to his parents, an irritant to his brother and a waste of space to his sister-in-law, but she liked him better than anyone she had encountered at Les Saules; better, indeed, than she could remember liking anyone for a long time.

On Friday she told Amèlie where she was going, in case Beth might have told her already. Amèlie looked beadily at her but said only, 'I'm sure you will find it very interesting.' Late in the afternoon she changed into the bright blue summer dress she had bought months ago at the market in Saumur. She felt excited, giggly, adolescent almost; and then, tugging a comb through her hair in front of the tiny rectangle of mirror, with no warning her old panic seized her. It was like being gripped by huge icy hands, crushing out her breath and turning her legs to marshmallow. She sat down, wrapping her arms round herself and trying to catch her breath while the sick, shaky feeling subsided. When she could breathe again she collapsed on the sofa and listened to the voice that had so abruptly dragged her back to her old self.

Aren't you being a bit, silly, dear? said Aunt Emily. *Getting all dolled up in an outfit suitable for a young girl and rushing off to chase some man ... do you actually think he'll believe you only want to hear the lecture?*

She was about to change the silly, girly dress for her old cords and a long shirt – something that couldn't possibly give the impression she thought of herself as, well, that she thought of herself at all. But just then she caught sight of the clock, and with no more time to think snatched up a jacket, stumbled outside, clumsily locked the door and set off for the train station at a run.

She reached the library with a few minutes to spare. The door to the meeting room was open and she peered inside. She could see rows of people sitting on the flimsy seats that can be found in adult education centres wherever you go. They all seemed to know each other and to be talking quietly together; she caught both English and French voices. Hervé couldn't have started yet, anyway. For a moment she was on the verge of turning back and going home, but just then another late arrival came and politely ushered her in, so she took a chair near the door.

Hervé was on a small platform at the end of the long room, in front of a screen and sitting to one side of a table looking through a pile of papers. She was briefly surprised to see a laptop and beamer on the same table, and then scolded herself for silliness; had she expected that a lecturer couldn't use the simplest technology? Just then he got up and started fumbling with the laptop, pressing keys apparently at random and looking from the keyboard to the screen and back again in a way that, even from the other end of the room, didn't inspire confidence. Gillian forgave herself.

After a few moments a calm middle-aged woman stepped onto the platform. She and Hervé exchanged a few words and the woman nodded, pressed keys and an image of the Chateau de Chenonceau appeared on the screen. Hervé squared the papers on the desk, came round to the front of it and began: '*Bonsoir, mesdames et messieurs* – good evening, ladies and gentlemen.' He explained briefly that the talk would be in French but the handout was available in English 'and an English friend has kindly corrected my mistakes, so I hope it will be clear', and if anyone had difficulties with the language he would try to help; Mme Trottier of the *cercle d'amitié* had just come to his rescue with the visuals, so they could now start.

'I'll begin with a description you may have heard before: "The Loire is a queen and kings have loved her." '

She was surprised at how different he was when he was doing something he understood. There was no sign of nervousness, that almost hunched, apologetic posture was gone, he looked straight at the audience and spoke without hesitation.

There was little that she couldn't follow in French, and where there was an obscure phrase it was usually followed by a paraphrase in English. Once or twice she recognised her own amendments to the original handout and felt a touch of pride.

Even with her very imperfect French, she could tell that the lecture was simplified for its audience: an hour's tour of the Loire for first-time visitors. But it was equally clear that Hervé loved the region and knew it intimately; listening to him and looking at the images on the screen, she was reminded of the way she had felt looking down from the roof of the castle at Chinon. Would it ever be possible to put it into her own words? to look back, as he could, at the length of the river and see all its past laid out along its wide, low banks: the wines and the wars, the bloodshed and the intrigues and the shimmering summer evenings?

There was applause, and there were questions; Hervé still seemed perfectly at ease. When the talk was finished and people were starting to make their way out, she saw that he was in conversation with his helper and two people who had been sitting near the platform: the organisers, she guessed. She got up and slipped out of the room among the others; she would have liked to say something about the talk, but could think of nothing that wouldn't sound silly and gushing or, much worse, patronising. Perhaps it would be best just to go home. She hoped he would come and visit her – his family, she meant of course – again while she was still there.

She had almost reached the outside door when she heard her name called, and turned to see Hervé hurrying after her and almost knocking over a couple who were strolling along the corridor.

'Gillienne' – he seemed to have got all his awkwardness back – 'I wanted to speak to you before you left. It was so good of you to come—'

'No, it was good of you to let me, and I enjoyed it a lot,' she said, thinking how stiff and unenthusiastic she must sound, but not knowing what else to say.

'Really? I'm very glad. But look, it was really your translation that made it … I mean, I would like to … I have to spend a little time with the people from the history society, otherwise I would … I mean, if you were free this evening ... ' The lecturer persona seemed to have been lost as completely as if he'd left it on a chair with his papers like a jacket.

'This evening?' Gillian was surprised.

He looked dejected. 'Yes, of course you have plans already. Well, perhaps some other—' he was edging back towards the hall.

'No!' she said, hoping it didn't come out as a squeak. 'No, I'm not busy at all.'

'You aren't? Then if, if you don't mind waiting a little, would you perhaps like to have dinner with me? I won't be long at all, and there's coffee in the lecture room ... '

'I'd love to! There's no hurry, I don't mind waiting at all. Now you'd better get back to your visitors and I'll see you in there.'

In fact he was hardly gone for ten minutes, though that was time enough for Aunt Emily to take over her thoughts again. Was he asking her out to be polite, because she'd helped him with the notes? Or worse, out of kindness to a slightly mad foreign lady who lived all alone in a field? And when had she ever spent an evening talking alone with anyone, let alone a man she hardly knew – how could she fail to be a bore and a disappointment?

But when he came hurrying in, apologising for keeping her waiting, all those fears vanished. He led her out through a side door, saying, 'The car park's this way.' Gillian hesitated. 'Are we going by car? It's just that I'll have to get back to the station later.'

Hervé looked appalled. 'No, of course you won't! I'll take you back to Les Châtres after dinner. In fact I was thinking we could go to a place in Cinq-Mars – you've been there, I suppose – and then I'll take you to Les Saules. Is that all right? I warn you now, though, I'm a terrible driver.'

She soon realised that this wasn't self-deprecation. The car was a little Clio and reminded her of her poor dead Micra – very easy to handle compared to the Trafic, she would have thought, but Hervé struggled with the gears and the pedals as if trying to subdue a bucking horse. She wondered if it would be rude to offer to drive another time, if there was another time.

They sat outdoors under apple trees; the sun was still up and when Gillian laid an arm against the stone wall she could feel its warmth. It struck her that gardens like this, exotic not long ago, had come to feel like home.

'It's lovely here,' she said to Hervé, 'it reminds me of your mother's garden.'

'Yes, a lot of places around here are like this.' He was anxiously studying the menu. 'If you've never tried brochet, Gillienne, I think you should.'

When they had ordered and Gillian had drunk some of the wine he had painstakingly chosen, she felt able to say, 'I did love your talk, Hervé. It, it seemed to say everything I've felt about this region somehow.'

'And what do you feel about the region?'

She looked a while into her glass. 'Maybe', she began slowly, 'it's just being in France, I don't know it well enough to tell. But there's something about being in a place where people drink their own wine, and eat what they grow …'

'You grew up in a village, didn't you? and here you're living in a town, even if it's a small one. Is it so very different in England? Apart from the wine, let's say …'

'I don't know,' she said, still unsure what she wanted to say. 'Yes, I lived in a village and of course it's the same in some ways. But … it might be because I'm an outsider. I get such a sense here of lives just going on, people living in this valley since prehistoric times, and just, oh, working the land and the vineyards and bringing up their families through Roman times and wars … perhaps that's why it feels so rich, so peaceful … I'm not making sense, am I?'

'Yes, you are. I understand what you mean, but I don't think peace exists anywhere that humans live. This is a rich land, certainly. That's why people have fought over it since the Romans at least. These castles the visitors love – they were all built as fortresses. And you can find as much cruelty, as much evil and suffering here as you can anywhere. There aren't any peaceful places, not when you look closely.'

'Of course, yes. I know I must just sound like a silly tourist, going on about "this lovely place" with no idea of what it's really like or what's happened in it. And I suppose I've seen very little of life.'

'Everyone, if you think about it, sees as much of life as everyone else, don't they? It all depends on what you mean by life and how much attention you're paying.'

'Yes … so when you look around here, let's say' – she gestured towards the quiet streets beyond the garden wall, and beyond them the meadows turning gold as the sun dropped – 'what do you see? All the wars and the, the bloodshed, and the treachery? Do you think being a historian makes you see the worst?'

'Yes ... no. The best and the worst, maybe. We humans just aren't very good at the business of living, are we?'

Gillian smiled a little. 'I thought that was only me.'

'Is that how you see yourself?'

She looked down into her glass again. 'I always have, yes. Not so much since I came here.'

'When we talked the other day,' he said, 'you told me how you suddenly decided to leave everything behind and come to France. And you said it meant so much to you, being here. But what is it that means so much?'

Gillian wasn't sure she understood. 'I mean,' he said, 'is it the work? The people? Living alone with no ties?'

'Oh, I see.' She sighed and took a sip of wine. She was beginning to drift, pleasantly. She had a hazy recollection of that evening with Greg in Hardelot. Here she was again, slowly getting tipsy with a stranger, telling her life story. But a different stranger and a different story. Or was it the same story, and only she had changed? 'I've been a coward all my life,' she said at last. 'Everything, everything that seemed to come so easily to other people, was like climbing a mountain to me. Learning to drive, coming into a room full of people, anything' – she glanced around the darkening garden – 'I was afraid of the dark, of driving, of being alone, of other people ...' It sounded so silly that she began to laugh.

Hervé didn't laugh. 'And then one day you decided to drive to a foreign country and travel through it on your own. What made you do that?'

'I just woke up in the middle of the night and decided I'd do it – and I did. It was that or just go on in the same way for ever, becoming a sour old woman like my aunt and some of her friends ... and once I got away from everything, Southash and my job and the people I'd known all my life, it all seemed easier. I ...' She came to a halt, stammering, 'Hervé, I – I'm so sorry, I'm just chattering on and on about myself, we were talking about the Loire and that's what—'

'I want to hear about you, Gillienne. You aren't used to talking about yourself, are you? You prefer to get other people to talk, I've noticed that. But I want to know about you, is that so hard to believe?'

'I suppose it is,' she said. 'I'm not used to it. There's nothing to know, you see. I don't think I've ever met anyone who's lived a duller life than I have.'

'So maybe that,' said Hervé, 'is why you seem to be perfectly happy here, with my family, living exactly the life I couldn't wait to escape from?'

'Yes, why not? I've felt useful for the first time in my life, I've been learning new things every day and I've been free. It would be different for you, wouldn't it? Expected to go into the family business – is that how it was?'

'Yes, it was expected. I'm not sure I've ever been forgiven.' He looked for a moment as if he wanted to say something more, and then instead smiled at her. You have the sweetest smile I've ever seen, she thought, and in another minute I'll have drunk enough to say so out loud.

'My aunt will never forgive me for leaving either.'

'She must be very fond of you,' Hervé suggested.

Gillian laughed. 'Oh no, I don't think she's fond of me at all. Well, perhaps in her way. But she had all the trouble of bringing me up, and I suppose she assumed I was always going to be there to look after her in her old age. Not that I won't be – I mean, she doesn't really need looking after yet.'

'Can I ask what happened to your parents?'

'My mother – I don't know anything about my father, not even who he was. It was on a ferry crossing from Dover to Ostend. The ferry ran aground – I've got an old newspaper cutting about it, but I don't know a lot of the details. I do know twenty-eight people were killed and, well, one of those was my mother.' She saw that Hervé was looking intently at her, and felt obscurely ashamed of being able to speak about it with so little feeling. 'I was very small, less than three years old; I've tried to remember her but I can't. She left me with my aunt – it was supposed to be a weekend trip. She, Aunt Emily I mean, didn't like talking about it – well, I can understand that. So I don't know much about my mother. But I do know she'd been working as a French teacher for a few years before she died. 'And' – for some reason it suddenly seemed important to tell him – 'she gave me a French name.'

'Gillienne – that's unusual in French too.'

'No, that's just the way everyone here pronounces Gillian. That's what I'm usually called, but my real name's Ghislaine.' She spelled it, stumbling over the letters.

'Ah, now that's a real old French name – though I think it was Germanic if you go back far enough. And you know what it means?'

'No – do you know, I've never even thought about it.'

'It means hostage or pledge – from when rich medieval families used to leave a child to be brought up in another household, as a kind of guarantee, to secure an alliance between the families.'

Just as well I didn't know that, Gillian thought. I was miserable enough without seeing myself as a hostage. I wonder if my mother knew what it meant?

The sun was down and it was growing cooler. It was all too easy to remember the cold dark house, the looming furniture that looked black in the twilight. She shivered.

'Are you cold, Gillienne – Ghislaine? We can go inside.'

'No, no, I'm not cold at all. But I suppose it is getting late.'

He looked round for the waiter and dug into his pocket at the same time. Gillian as quickly dived for her shoulder bag, but he gestured no. 'I invited you here and I will pay, of course. No, put your money away.'

Gillian was wholly unused to being taken out, but it seemed more polite to give in than to insist – and for all she knew about French dining etiquette, it could even be quite insulting not to let him pay. For the second time she was reminded of Greg and his expense account, but this was clearly a very different thing. Besides, she didn't have nearly enough money on her.

He pulled up in the lane behind the meadow, rather than the road in front of the house. 'Can I leave you here, Ghislaine? I won't go in the house now, it's late.'

Indeed she was surprised how late it was. Amèlie might well have gone to bed, though she could see at least one light on.

'Hervé,' she said, 'I had such a lovely time.'

He turned towards her. 'You mean it? I don't know if you have any time this weekend?'

Yes, she wanted to shout. Aloud she said, 'I've got to help tomorrow, but what about Sunday?'

Even in the dim street light she could see his smile. 'Sunday – yes! I'd like to show you Orléans – well, we can decide all that later. If I come here ... is ten too early?'

No, she said, ten wasn't too early. She reached for the door handle and then, trying to copy what she supposed a Frenchwoman would do, leaned across and kissed him awkwardly and formally on the cheek. He lifted a hand to touch her face and kissed her very gently on the mouth. For a second they stayed still and then, not knowing how to respond, what to do, she drew slowly away and said, 'Goodnight, Hervé, I'll be ready at ten, and thank you, thank you so much for this evening.'

When he had driven away she stayed in the lane for a moment. You're crazy, she told herself, you've been on your own too long; it's just saying goodnight for god's sake. But looking back along the road she ached for him to be still with her, and when she opened the gate her hands were shaking. She crossed the patch of grass, unlocked the van and switched on the light. The routine actions were soothing and she began to think more clearly. Why hadn't she asked him in? Was that what people did? What about Sunday, what would she ...

There was no time to think further. She heard rapid footsteps on the path, a rattle as someone tugged at the gate and, astonished, opened the door just as Amèlie reached it.

'Gillienne' – it was too dark to read her expression, but her voice was anxious – 'I've been looking out for your light. You've had a call from a friend in England; I think the name was Kate. She couldn't speak much French but she said it was urgent, I understood that. Do you want to come to the house and call her now?'

Kate greeted her with: 'So you finally bothered to call.'

'I've been out, Kate, what's the matter?'

'Gill, your Aunt Emily is ill.'

'Ill, what do you mean?'

'She had a stroke two days ago. Haven't you got any of my emails?'

Gillian sat down at the desk, feeling very sick. She drew a shaky breath. 'I ... Kate, I haven't looked, I've been so busy ...' Feeble, feeble excuses. What you mean is, I've been enjoying myself so much, and lately I've been spending every free moment thinking about a man I hardly even know—

'Well, however *busy* you may be, I suggest you come home as fast as you can. Do you think you could manage that? Or are you *too* busy?' She stopped abruptly. Gillian heard her take a breath. 'I'm sorry, Gill, it's not your fault. But it's all fallen on me, trying to reach you, and dealing with the hospital. I had to go in the house and look through her things just to find this number. None of her so-called friends have been the least use. And then when it looked like you couldn't even be bothered to read your emails – you were supposed to check them every day, weren't you?'

Gillian forced herself to focus. 'Kate, I'm coming straight home, of course I am. But it's such a shock. It must have come so suddenly: I've spoken to her most weeks and she hasn't said anything about not being well.'

'Well, from what she told me, you were doing so well and having such a good time she didn't like to worry you. But she hasn't been well all summer.' Kate's voice was less unfriendly now. 'And I didn't think she looked well either, but you know what she's like – when I saw her she always said she was fine.' It wasn't like Aunt Emily to be so considerate. On the other hand, not making a fuss over illness was certainly part of her creed. 'I asked her once if she didn't need anyone to help in the house – you arranged someone, didn't you? and she was adamant that she didn't need help.'

Yes, Gillian remembered Emily saying the same thing to her. She remembered too that in their last calls she had seemed ... odd. Abstracted. And she, not wanting anything to disturb her in her new life, had been happy to take no notice, to assume that the tough old woman was still as strong as she had always been, that she was, as she kept claiming, perfectly all right on her own.

Anyway, what mattered now was getting home as fast as possible. 'Kate, I'll take the first tunnel crossing and be back by midday tomorrow – and thank you, thank you – you've been wonderful.'

When she went into the kitchen Amèlie looked at her with concern. 'My dear, you are very pale. Sit down and I'll get you something to drink.'

'No, thank you, Amèlie, I'm all right.' She slumped in a chair and fought for words. 'It's just that my aunt is very ill and I'll have to, I'll have to—' She was close to tears, and hating herself for it; because Amèlie, full of sympathy, believed she was desperately worried about a beloved guardian, and Gillian knew she was only overcome with despair because she had to go home.

13: Rain

Gillian left her aunt's room, trying to move as unobtrusively as she had seen the nurse do. She failed, but Emily had fallen asleep again and didn't stir. Reaching the big, heavily furnished living room where the two of them used to sit through interminable evenings, Gillian fell into a chair by the window and closed her eyes.

Only a week since she had left Les Châtres. Impossible to believe. Already the journey through France, the weeks by the Loire were like a fantasy, a story she might once have told herself to help her get through the day. *One day I'll just walk out of here and I'll have a little place of my own by the river ...*

The drive back to Calais had been uneventful. How easy everything seemed, now that she would – secretly, ashamedly – have welcomed any kind of delay. After a frenzied effort to get everything secured and ready for the journey home, she took the dreaded autoroute without even thinking. The only real difficulty had been finding her direction back from the Folkestone roundabout, but even that didn't worry her. Driving on the left again felt strange, the more so in the left-hand drive Trafic, but England itself looked so odd after the months in the Loire Valley that she hardly thought about it. She drove along the motorway in the comparative quiet of the early hours, marvelling at the narrowness of the lanes, the bright green of the countryside and the ubiquity of roadworks. Had this strange, cramped land with its pinkish-grey light always been her home? And did it have to welcome her with quite so much rain? She half wondered if it had ever stopped since the day she left.

Aunt Emily was supposedly out of danger. Her speech no longer slurred and, although she was convinced that she now looked like a monster, the dropping of the left side of her face was barely visible. But she was permanently exhausted, dozing or lying still for most of the day, and in the lowest of spirits when she was awake. She had grown fearful of being alone, calling out if Gillian left her for more than a few minutes.

'This is all quite normal in stroke patients,' the nurse had told her, 'once Auntie's up and about she'll soon be feeling more cheerful.'

Well, they would just have to see. At any rate Aunt Emily seemed to be sleeping peacefully at the moment. It would do her good, and there was nearly an hour before it would be time to start preparing dinner. Gillian wanted badly just to stay in the chair and doze off too, but this might be her only chance to call Les Saules and tell them why she wouldn't be back for a while.

Amèlie answered. Hearing her cool, clear voice, even hearing French spoken, brought Gillian such a wave of emotion that she almost choked as she began, 'Amèlie, it's me, Gillienne; I'm sorry I couldn't call before.' There was a tiny pause and then the dialling tone. Puzzled, Gillian dialled again; they must have been cut off. This time she got the engaged signal.

All right, she would have to try again in a little while. She went back to the chair and tried to get comfortable, but it was designed for people of an earlier era to sit bolt upright on and pass tight-lipped judgment on their neighbours, not for spineless creatures like herself to loll and dream in. After a few minutes she gave up, went to the table and took the phone again. She was restless now; whatever was wrong with the connection, she would keep trying unless Aunt Emily woke up again. It would be so good to speak to them all again, even if there was no chance of going back for a while ...

'*Âllo?*' This time it was Beth, in her heavily accented French. 'Beth! It's Gillian. I got cut off just now. I called to ask how you all are and—' becoming aware that Beth had said nothing since the first word, she ended lamely, 'and, well, what's been happening.'

Pause. Then, 'You want to know what's been happening, do you? And why exactly would we tell you?'

Gillian thought she must have heard wrong. 'Whatever do you mean?' she managed at last.

'Just how much have you written about us, Gillian? After the first article? What is it now, a series? I'm sure we gave you lots to write about – especially me, being the fool that I am, thinking we were friends and telling you everything. But it's not just me. Amèlie's so upset she can't even talk to you. That's why she put the phone down on you and asked me to answer it if you called again.'

Gillian listened, feeling colder and sicker with every word. Of course, she had asked Beth to open any post that came for her. So the magazine had come with the article in it – that sarcastic sketch of a comic Anglo-French family, written in that, yes, *petulant* mood that had overtaken her when she realised that, after accepting her help for one evening, they wanted no more of her.

'Nothing to say?' said Beth. 'I suppose you're saving it all.'

Gillian found her voice. 'Beth, it was one sketch, it was just because all the next day I was thinking about you all and—'

'Oh, leave it. I mean, who's going to read it anyway?' Perhaps realising that she could hardly better that last shot, Beth seemed to lose interest. 'Anyway, I hope you haven't got any more post coming because I really haven't time to deal with it, and you may as well know I've thrown out your address. Right then—'

'Wait! Let me speak to Amèlie, I need to explain …'

'Amèlie isn't well' – there was a definite hint of gloating – 'and your call made her worse. She's lying down.'

'Oh no, I'm so sorry !' Sensing the receiver about to crash down, she stammered out, 'What about Hervé, surely he—'

'Hervé's seen the article all right. Well, he had to know why his mum was so upset, didn't he? Obviously, now he realises you were only all over him so you could pick his brains for a bit of local colour – I don't know what happened with you two, but he looked as sick as a parrot and we haven't seen him since. It's quite a gift you've got, isn't it, Gillian, getting people to talk? If that's all you did?'

Gillian could only repeat, in a whisper, 'I'm so sorry.'

'Yes, I'm sure you are. Bye then.'

She slumped in the chair and stared out of the window. Rain poured from the gutters and splashed across the paving slabs. Looking out over the drenched lawn she had a flash of memory: herself as a child of five, creeping out to play in this garden on a rainy day without shoes or a coat, and being caught by her aunt. Emily had glared at her and said, 'Well, if you like it so much you can stay there' and gone back inside and slammed the door. Gillian had tugged and tugged at the door but it wouldn't open. The rain had started to hurl down as it was doing now, torrents and buckets of it, and she had cried in terror and desolation for what seemed like hours. It was probably no more than five minutes; but as she looked out now she felt the cold wet grass on her bare feet and the water pouring down her neck.

14: Emily

After a while Aunt Emily left her room and began, slowly but with determination, to renew her grip on life, her niece's as well as her own.

She was as autocratic as ever and her mind seemed unaffected, except that she would sometimes find herself unable to remember a word or phrase. But she was constantly tense, calling out in the night convinced that someone was trying to break in, unwilling to let Gillian leave the house even for a short time.

Still unsteady on her feet and easily tired, she had no choice but to let Gillian do all the work of running the house, but supervised her as if she had been a child of ten, not trusting her even with tasks she had been doing for years. She would come into a room as soon as Gillian had cleaned it, poking at ornaments too heavy for her to lift and peering at surfaces, hoping to see finger marks. Cooking was the worst, for Emily would come into the dark north-facing kitchen to sit upright in the one chair, instructing her in the simplest steps and telling her to do things just as she was about to do them anyway.

In her stolen moments alone, Gillian would open her laptop and, with one eye on the door, try to find websites and links that might tell her what to do, how long things were likely to stay like this. As far as she could discover her aunt wasn't ill enough to need a full-time carer, so as long as Gillian stayed with her there would be no other help forthcoming.

And maybe it was true, as far as it went, that she didn't need any other care. She was soon able to dress herself, move around the house and even as far as the front gate, though she refused to go any further. She ate well enough, though she was endlessly critical of Gillian's cooking, and generally seemed, in the nurse's faintly annoying phrase, to be 'quite well in herself'.

But there were no assessments to cover the fact that she was, under the carping manner, a bewildered old woman who seemed in permanent dread of something unseen; or that her niece found herself unable to be brisk and practical with her. No doubt Aunt Emily could safely be left on her own for a few hours, but she refused to believe it, and the one time Gillian stayed out for an afternoon instead of hurrying home after doing the shopping and errands, her reproaches lasted for days. It wasn't worth it.

Gillian had got as far as dialling the number of Les Saules once more, but her nerve failed her as soon as the ringtone started and she hung up. She emailed, and then wrote to Amèlie by post, but wasn't surprised when there was no reply. Would she have felt so differently in their place? And in a way she *had* used them. Although after the first article she had never written another word about them, their characters, the way the *pension* was run and the whole atmosphere of the place had, almost without her knowing it, coloured the sketches and tentative stories she had scribbled since.

But she hadn't used Hervé, and that he should believe otherwise was unbearable. At first, on the nights when she couldn't sleep, she tried searching for him, but there was no Facebook profile, not a mention anywhere except that he was named as giving a lecture five years back to some local society, with no contact details; and as one of the named authors on a journal paper with no public access. She remembered the handwritten notes and the frantic tussle with PowerPoint; he was hardly more at home with modern media than Amèlie. And why should he be, when his real world, the one he lived in, was a dream of the Loire's past?

It wouldn't be that hard to track him down, she supposed, staring dull-eyed at the screen, but what good would it do? Was she going to email him or what? *Dear Hervé, you may remember that we spent an evening together last August. I had to leave France unexpectedly the next day as my aunt was ill. You may have heard from Beth that I published a magazine article ...*

What could she say, even if she could find him? *I wasn't just looking for something to write about, please believe me, I miss you so much but I can't come to France now, could you, would you ...?* And now it was already three o'clock and Aunt Emily would wake at six as had been her lifelong habit, and her demands would not cease from that moment, and Gillian was tired, tired.

The days passed with little change. As winter came closer Aunt Emily seemed to shrink again; it grew harder to persuade her to go outside for a while, to take even a vague interest in the garden or the news from the village. As little as she had ever mixed with her neighbours, there had been the few lifelong friends, the ancient vicar she still looked down on as a boy; but she shunned such visits and help as were offered. 'Let Mrs Joyce stay with you while I'm out,' Gillian urged at first. 'So she can sit pretending to be full of sympathy and then go and spread the news of how Emily Bailie is a dribbling old cripple now? Oh yes, she'd enjoy that. She was always spiteful.'

'You don't dribble, you aren't a cripple and I thought she was supposed to be your oldest friend.'

'Don't answer me back, girl!'

Gillian found herself laughing. 'Aunt Emily, you do remember how old I am, don't you?'

Emily looked malevolently at her and fell into brooding silence. Gillian knew her well enough to have a good idea what she was thinking; since 'that silly French trip' it must seem to her that her niece was no longer the person who had gone away. Without ever putting it into words, even to herself, she had rather liked the fact that Gillian was so easily cowed, so anxious for approval and so unsure that she could ever gain it. She took it as a tribute to the way she had brought 'the girl' up. Her one-time friends – those spiteful old women from whose sharp eyes she was now hiding – had sometimes complimented her on the excellent job she had done, giving the wayward Rose's daughter a proper traditional upbringing.

But the subdued and frightened child, who had seemed always to remain a child, had gone and now there was this suntanned woman with her bold voice and her movements full of energy, who looked after her former guardian and nagged her, and most intolerable, laughed at her.

Still, as the days stretched into weeks, the boldness and the energy were fading along with the tan. And after the conversation with Beth Gillian no longer saw much to laugh at, in Aunt Emily's oddities or anything else. She started to wear her old clothes again, since it was too cold for her new ones and there seemed no point in buying anything, not to mention the fact that she was still earning no money.

That September the papers were full of stories about the collapse of a bank she had hardly heard of; the TV news showed lines and lines of people rushing to get their savings out of it, and suddenly all the neighbours were worrying about their own nest eggs and talking about what to do if their own banks and building societies went the way of Northern Rock. Gillian watched and listened with no particular interest beyond a faint, malicious amusement that so many people she knew who had always claimed to be penniless were now panicked that the government wouldn't guarantee savings above £50,000. Well, she thought, at least I don't have to worry about that. She was finding it increasingly hard to think or care about the outside world, or anything much beyond the tasks and anxieties and annoyances that each day brought.

The day she sold the Trafic was the day she finally accepted the way things were now. The buyers were a couple in their twenties with a small daughter, overjoyed to think they would now be able to afford holidays abroad.

The little girl went straight to try out her 'room', the space under the roof that Gillian had used as storage, and hung over the edge breathless with excitement while her parents peered and prodded and opened doors, and turned back to Gillian with queries about waste water and gas supplies and all the mysteries that she found so simple now. The only hard question was 'Won't you miss it?' which made her flinch and pretend not to hear. With the sale money she bought a Ford Fiesta hardly younger than the long-lost green Micra; for the journeys she would be making, it was more than adequate.

As she had done all her life, she lived her days according to routine. There was the overlarge house to look after, meals to be shopped for and prepared, appointments to organise for the physio, Aunt Emily's well-being to see to and her endless demands to be met. Once or twice she managed to persuade Emily to let a neighbour sit with her while she went to visit Kate or just go for a walk, but more often it was Kate who came to her.

'You're looking ill,' Kate told her one afternoon in November, as they sat talking in low voices while Aunt Emily dozed in her room. 'When you got back from France you looked great – I hardly recognised you—'

'Thanks,' muttered Gillian with a faint flicker of amusement.

'Well, you know what I mean. Now you've lost too much weight and you're peaky. How long do you think you can go on being at her beck and call day and night?'

Gillian sighed and looked out over the garden. Even in its well-tended prime and on a sunny day, it was a depressing place with its regimented rows of plants and dark, secret hedges. Now, dejected and scruffy under a dirty sky, it seemed so perfect a mirror of her own state that she almost laughed at the clichéd aptness of it.

'Are you listening, Gill?'

She turned back to Kate and gave her a weary smile. 'Oh yes, I'm listening but what can I do? They tell me Aunt Emily isn't ill enough to qualify for any other help, but she isn't well enough to be left alone for long and there's only me. She won't even see her friends, not that she ever had many; but she's getting a bit better. I suppose she'll be able to stay on her own for longer soon.'

'Yes, but she won't be able to live alone, will she? Are you just going to stay with her for the rest of her life? And what will you live on if you can't go back to work?'

Gillian sighed again. It was all true, she knew it, and on the nights when she couldn't sleep all these things went round and round in her head, but she was so tired, Kate couldn't know how tired she was …

She pulled herself upright and tried to concentrate. 'I have wondered about trying to find a job,' she said, 'but what is there around here? I was thinking about working from home though, being a virtual assistant or something. But it's finding the time without being interrupted; it's almost like having a baby. Well, *you* know—'

'I'd rather have two more babies and go through it all again than your auntie,' said Kate, too loudly. Gillian looked nervously towards the door, but it was shut. Kate laughed. 'Do her good,' she began, but lowered her voice in response to Gillian's expression. 'Gill, you always did let her bully you and you're doing it again. If you're going to stay and look after her you've got to make some rules; she's not a complete invalid. And – look, I know it sounds harsh, but it's not as if she was ever that nice to you, is it?'

Gillian considered this for a while. 'I think she was as nice as she knew how to be. She didn't have to bring me up, did she? She could have just put me in a home or something. At any rate I can't let her down now. You must see that.'

'Yes, I suppose so. Listen, I've got more time now Martha's starting reception class, and you know I was going to start looking for a job soon anyway. Why don't I come and stay with Emily for a couple of hours now and then? You can pay me a bit as soon as you find something yourself.'

Gillian was deeply touched. She wondered how to tell her friend, 'But Aunt Emily doesn't like you.'

'That's a lovely idea, Kate,' she said cautiously, 'but I'm not sure how Aunt Emily would feel about imposing on you like that.'

'Well, you can tell her,' said Kate, 'that it's me or a stranger. If you go on like this you'll be needing a carer yourself, not to mention running out of money.' She got up. 'Anyway, you think it over.'

Gillian did think about it for a while, though without much hope. She even tried, very gently, to pass on Kate's suggestion to Emily, but met such a blank wall that, for now at least, she gave up. Then, two days later, an email arrived.

Dear Gillian,

Thank you for your article, 'Lost in France', which we have decided to publish in our November issue. We would also be interested in seeing further work from you.

She sat looking at the words over and over. She was going to be published, in print, *for money*. And they wanted more! For the first time in months, she felt energy, excitement; she couldn't sit still, she jumped up and was about to rush from the room when another thought hit her. The article that had caused all the trouble, the one about Les Saules – wouldn't she have been paid for that? By cheque, probably, as surely no one had asked for her bank details. No doubt an envelope had arrived, only to be binned by Beth or Amèlie.

She sat down again. Her friends the Martins already saw her as a heartless user, a vampire preying on the emotions of real people with real lives. And they were probably right at that. Well then, she might as well get as much blood as she could. She'd start by writing to the other magazine and telling them how it was that she had never received the news that her sketch was being published, let alone the payment. And then she would reply to this one and tell them – well, she would tell them both – that there would definitely be more work – no, she would suggest something. An outline, an idea for a series?

She was busy writing when Aunt Emily began calling for her afternoon cup of tea. She made it absentmindedly, and when her aunt grumbled that it wasn't brewed enough, laughed and said, 'Never mind, Auntie, think of all the starving children.'

Emily looked suspiciously at her over the cup. 'Have you been drinking?' she demanded. 'Gillian laughed again. 'Have I – it's four in the afternoon! I never start before five, you know that. Shall I make shepherd's pie tonight?'

'Well, you look as if something had happened. You're quite flushed. I hope you aren't coming down with something.'

Gillian smiled and looked down at her own cup. She had a moment's impulse to tell Emily what had happened; but she knew it would be madness. Even if her aunt didn't simply set herself against it, five minutes of her candid criticism would leave Gillian afraid to touch the keyboard again. She would be a vampire and feed in secret … What about a series on caring for an elderly relative with stroke? An annoying elderly relative about whom you couldn't preface complaints with 'Much as I love her' because you didn't and never had? It occurred to her that in all the blogs and articles and interviews she had ever read about the lives of carers – and in the last two months she had seen hundreds – not one had ever taken that angle. It was always assumed, by bloggers and commenters alike, that the patient was somebody you loved, or at the very least used to love.

'No, I'm fine, really. Shepherd's pie then?'

'No, thank you,' said Aunt Emily, 'you always overcook the mince and you don't mash the potato enough. It was full of lumps last time.'

'We'll have whatever you fancy then, Auntie,' cooed Gillian. Would she use a pseudonym? Or wouldn't she bother?

'And don't call me Auntie.'

'Whatever you fancy, Aunt Emily.' No, she wouldn't bother.

15: Words

By January Gillian's blog had quite a following. 'Diary of an Uncaring Carer' drew furious tirades, religious exhortation and sympathy in about equal amounts. In the end she had decided to call herself Lia and Emily, in a pleasingly petty little revenge, was Auntie, but apart from some tweaking for comic effect, she stuck quite closely to the detail of their lives.

Her early posts tried to be light-hearted, but she soon found that when she lost patience and used the blog as an outlet for her suppressed rage, she got more response. *I've been the sole carer for my elderly mother for two years*, one woman wrote. *I constantly feel like a monster because I'm so full of resentment at being left alone to care for her with no thanks and no help. You say everything I want to say and I don't feel so alone now.*

She was becoming aware of a world of people, mostly women, mostly older than herself but sometimes much younger, dragging out a twilit existence that made her own life seem like one long adventure holiday. She got posts from people who never left their homes except in an emergency, who saw no one from week to week except for the dementia-ravaged spouse or parent they struggled to feed, to keep clean, to give some semblance of a decent life long after everything that made life worth living was gone.

She became aware that in this new country, she was among the happiest and the most privileged of citizens. It was shame at having, comparatively, so little to complain of that first made her start to exaggerate Emily's symptoms and her cantankerousness. Then the relief, the secret feeling of power it gave her, grew irresistible. Gradually she turned her aunt into a caricature, a Victorian monster, with the health officials they occasionally saw cast as Dickensian grotesques and herself as a downtrodden, colourless drudge in the background.

That part was true anyway, she reflected, reading over one post before submitting. It seemed so much easier just to smile and give in, and later take her secret revenge through the keyboard, than to assert herself and set boundaries and all the other stuff she had never learned to do, but which Kate was so fond of assuring her would be easy once she started. Once or twice even Kate had found her way into the saga, though Gillian usually ended up deleting her bossiest remarks. Kate meant well, after all. So, most of the time, had Emily. If only people would stop meaning things, or just go away and leave her alone …

She had written to the first magazine and told them that she wasn't travelling any more, but was in England looking after her elderly aunt, who could no longer live alone, and that she was writing a blog about that. She sent them a link and supposed that would be the end of it, but before long another email came, along with a second cheque for the original article and a request for her bank details.

They liked her blog and wanted her to use it as the basis for a series of articles on the plight of the modern carer. Gillian barely hesitated before accepting. Aunt Emily never read magazines, and certainly not magazines aimed at women, for which she had a hearty contempt. Besides, it was always Gillian who fetched the post.

She settled into another routine. It wasn't hard to do her writing in the afternoons while Emily slept, or late in the evening after she had gone to bed. She began to look forward to her writing time as the only bright hours of the day.

Kate pointed out to her, one late winter afternoon, that Emily was getting better. 'Do you need to stay with her all the time now? Couldn't she manage, if you arranged some care and came back, at weekends say?'

Gillian was taken aback. Since refusing Kate's earlier offer of help, and especially after finding the release of writing, she had simply resigned herself to life in this prison and not looked beyond the walls. But thinking about it, yes: as usual, Kate was right. Her aunt now walked independently, managed to eat and wash and dress with no great difficulty and was capable of managing her affairs. She might still keep a frantic grip on her niece's movements, declaring herself unable to be left alone; but it was quite possible that, if she actually were left alone with some part-time help, she might even be the better for it.

Only. Only.

Gillian walked aimlessly around the garden after Kate left, stooping to pull up a weed now and then in case Emily was peering out of a window to catch her idling. Not surprising, perhaps, that she had fallen into this way of life and stopped thinking about it, but why, when a way out was offered to her, didn't she welcome it? Why did she instinctively shrink from the idea of freedom?

She chewed on the question for the rest of the day, and the answer came to her, as everything did lately, in the early hours when she couldn't sleep. She didn't want freedom because there was nothing she wanted to do with it. What was the use of leaving this cage to go and choose a slightly larger one? With Emily needing her near, it was no longer feasible to go off exploring as she had done in France – and besides, she had lost all heart for that.

She wondered what Kate was expecting her to do if she did leave. Go to speed-dating evenings, no doubt, train for a better job, take up zumba – god knew. Kate, she thought with a faint smile, just doesn't get it; she persists in treating me as if I was like other people.

The thought led to another: why aren't I like other people? Even when she was young she'd never had the luxury of teenage angst, of solemnly telling friends, 'I don't fit in', 'I don't conform' and all the rest of the rituals by which the young prove themselves so very much alike. She remembered listening to conversations like that, and wondering what it felt like to be so sure of your place in the world, so bored with being *normal* that you could find pleasure in denying it.

It was after five now. She got out of bed, put on her dressing-gown and, moving noiselessly through long habit, went downstairs. Her laptop was on the dining table but she made no move to switch it on, though this had become as much a part of her nightly routine as the early waking. She felt her way to the window seat and knelt up on it, pushing aside the heavy old curtains.

Under a three-quarter moon the garden lost its primness. The shadows of yew tree and laurel bush were black on the blue grass; alien and yet deeply, inevitably familiar. This was where she had always lived, in this cold blue world untouched by sun or rain. She had no more substance than the blue-black shadows; she was hollow at the core. At best she could only pretend to feel as real people did: laugh when they laughed, try to look as if she cared when they cried. What had she done, when she had the chance to live among real people, make real friendships? Turned them into her puppets, created a private world where they danced at her pleasure. Hadn't that been the attraction from the start, first the van and then Les Saules? A series of shadow houses where she could play at being, yes, a real person. And now in the largest, darkest house of all, she was playing at being a devoted carer.

'And now what?' she asked the world on the other side of the glass. Whether she stayed on in the dark house that had enclosed her for so long – whether she stayed until, like Emily, she had no more power to leave than a toy to jump out of its box – or whether she walked out now on stiff doll's legs to search for a new box: what difference would it make?

The first splinters of light were showing. A movement caught her eye. A cat had jumped onto the garden wall and was creeping along it, sniffing at something in the bush that grew up to its edge. The first bird sounded and the cat stiffened into alertness. It's alive, she thought, everything out there is alive. If that bird gets killed by the cat, it's still had more life than I have.

Then the absurdity of her self-pity struck her and she gave a little snort of laughter. She might write something about these before-dawn driftings – or would she? There had been all too many of them lately, and each time it was harder and harder to come back.

She found a sheet of paper and began scribbling without any conscious intention. After a while she looked at her handwriting, more erratic than ever in the half light. She had scrawled some irregular lines:

We're in a valley
can't reach the river
trapped in the dry valley
I can't see over the wall
can't reach the river
can't see over the wall

Presently she went back to her room, dressed and took Aunt Emily a cup of tea as usual. She wasn't aware of any change in her manner, but this morning Emily looked closely at her. She said nothing, but all through the day she seemed to be watching her, as if trying to confirm something. Preoccupied and listless from lack of sleep, Gillian made no attempt to find out what the problem was; no doubt Emily was getting ready to tell her that the curtains needed washing or the hedge cutting.

That evening they were sitting at the heavy dining table that Emily insisted on her fully laying each evening. Gillian had little appetite, but she had been trained from her earliest years to eat whatever was on her plate; she pushed her way stolidly through scrag end and gravy and, as she had also been trained to do, spoke only when spoken to.

It was Emily who broke the silence, just as Gillian got up to clear the table.

'You don't look well,' she said abruptly, 'is anything wrong?'

Gillian was startled into dropping a fork. Surprising her further, Aunt Emily failed to rebuke her for clumsiness but repeated, 'Is anything wrong?'

'No,' Gillian said, 'why should anything be wrong? Shall I get some—'

'No, sit down a minute, Gillian. I want to talk to you.'

Gillian sat down and waited. For once Aunt Emily seemed to be unsure what she wanted to say. After a while she went on: 'I know it hasn't been easy for you all these months. You've done a lot for me, Gillian, and' – the discomfort was palpable – 'I'm grateful.' Gillian made a faint sound of repudiation, but Emily waved her into silence. 'I expect I could manage on my own now, for a while at any rate, but …'

The crisp, arrogant voice faltered on a note of frightened old age. Looking at the bleak face opposite her, Gillian was moved almost to tears. After a moment Emily straightened her spine as she always had before making any effort, and went on: 'I'm leaving you everything, you know. No, don't say anything. I don't have much besides the house but you'll manage.

'You're a good girl, Gillian. I know I can trust you to take care of this house when I'm gone, and not let it out to incomers or do something dreadful with it. I shall be glad to think of you living here.'

Gillian could find nothing at all to say. She felt cold all over. Her eyes shifted from her aunt's face to the window behind her, as if bars had suddenly appeared on it and the door locked fast. After a long pause, in a very small voice she began, 'Aunt Emily, I don't —'

Emily waved speech impatiently away, and got up with a briskness she hadn't shown for a long time. 'Never mind, never mind. We won't talk about it again. I think I'll have an early night.' She said this every evening as if proposing a novelty, though she always went to bed straight after dinner.

Later Gillian went to her laptop, logged in to her blog and sat reading over the posts she had written and the articles she had sketched out. The resentment that had fuelled them was, at least for now, dulled by guilt, and she was appalled by what she had done. Her night thoughts had been right; she was a monster, incapable of human kindness. Here was what she had written only a week ago, annoyed by Emily's gloating over the death of a neighbour:

Auntie rather cheery today, mainly because one of her oldest friends has died. Nothing lifts her spirits like a funeral. Not quite up to going herself, but one of the village matriarchs popped in to tell her all about it so she wouldn't feel she'd missed the fun. Stayed two hours and between them they raked up every annoying thing the dear departed ever

'Gillian, about what I was saying … what is this?' Gillian swung round, leapt up and almost knocked into a dressing-gowned Aunt Emily, who was peering at the page. Her wits completely scattered, she didn't think to hide the screen until it was too late; Emily pushed her outstretched hand aside with surprising vigour, took her seat and read the page in silence.

She looked up at her niece and repeated her question. Her eyes looked more prominent than usual and you could see the veins on her forehead. Gillian, reading over her shoulder in cold horror, said, 'Auntie – Aunt Emily, don't get upset, it's nothing, just a sort of, um, diary to pass the time …'

Aunt Emily gave her a long, hard look and turned back to the screen. 'A diary that's published? Out there for all to see? And' – her eyes, racing over the page, reached the comments section – 'people *talk* about it?' Her voice grew thicker; her face was darkening. 'Have you been writing ... all this time ... for everyone to ... 'She talked on, but now it was impossible to understand what she was saying.

16: The Dark House

The wake was held in the church hall and was very modest – a rare case of the bereaved knowing, with absolute certainty, what the departed would have wished. Tea and biscuits and old ladies and the vicar; it was, Gillian reflected, probably as close as Aunt Emily had ever got to an orgy. She made a mental note of the sentence for an article, and then winced away from the idea.

Arranging the funeral and the catering had been quite easy. At first Kate had come forward, ready as ever to organise and instruct, but Gillian had lived nearly all her life among old people in a small community; funerals were among the few things of which she could claim plenty of experience.

Besides, her lifelong dread of being inefficient, of publicly failing to cope, was so wholly gone that she could barely even remember how it felt to be afraid of little things. The journey through France and the weeks of learning new skills in Les Châtres had taught her to rely on herself. And after the slow, exhausting months alone with Emily she could only wonder how she had ever found enough energy to worry about other people's expectations.

Especially now that she was a murderer. Was a murderer going to be consumed with guilt about not providing enough sandwiches for the victim's mourners? Another half-formed line for the blog; another shudder.

'You're coping wonderfully, dear,' said stately Mrs Joyce, who had patronised Gillian through her childhood and whom she had never yet dared call by her first name. 'And so organised too. Emily would be proud of you.'

'Thank you,' Gillian said. 'Can I get you something to drink?'

'No, thank you, dear; just sit down and talk to me a moment.' Gillian obediently sat, but she had never talked to Mrs Joyce in her life and doubted that she would need to begin now. Sure enough, after a sigh or two Mrs Joyce started.

'Your aunt and I were at school together, you know.' If Gillian didn't it was not for lack of being told. 'Not many of us left now who remember the old village, before they built that estate, and when we still had the shop and … ah well, never mind. But Emily always kept her house just the way her parents liked it – your grandparents, dear, though of course you never knew them.' Another hefty sigh. 'You don't see many houses like that nowadays. I do hope you'll be keeping it on, Gillian, and not selling it off to—' 'Incomers,' Gillian interrupted a village elder, possibly for the first time in her life.

Mrs Joyce looked pleased and leaned benevolently towards her. 'Well, yes, dear. There are so many new people here now, some of them – well, from anywhere in the world, though of course,' she dropped her voice as though secret police were lurking behind the trestle tables, 'you're not supposed to say anything. How lovely it will be to have a young person like you living here, someone who *understands* the village. You know Emily always did so much for the church …'

Gillian sat on, nodding now and then with a half-smile. How brief it had been, that dream of going out into the world as real people did, walking under the sky.

'…funny to think of it now, but Emily had all sorts of plans when we were girls. She wanted to go off travelling, but then of course your grandmother got ill, and Rose – your mother, I mean of course, dear, was still young and your grandfather couldn't manage everything by himself. Men can't, you know, I don't care what they say nowadays. Yes, she was a good girl, a good daughter. Mind you, they weren't easy, either of them, though I shouldn't say that. Made life very hard for poor Emily sometimes. Of course you don't remember either of them, do you?'

No, Gillian didn't. 'And I never knew Aunt Emily wanted to travel, she never mentioned it.'

Mrs Joyce's expression changed as she remembered that Gillian was not a contemporary to gossip with, but a junior who needed keeping in her place. 'No, well, in our day we didn't whine when we couldn't get what we wanted. And she'd hardly buried her parents when she lost her sister as well, and the next thing she knew she had you to bring up; so there wouldn't be much point in thinking about herself, would there?'

'No,' Gillian said softly, 'there wouldn't be much point.' She got up with a vague smile and, leaving Mrs Joyce to savour the memory of her friend's joyless existence, went to look again at the few photographs of Emily that she'd managed to get together for a display board. Thinking of what she had just heard, she looked more closely now at the old picture of the two sisters that had always been kept in Emily's room. They had been quite alike, Rose darker and livelier, but yes, you could see that Emily had been young once. In one of the pictures she was even laughing; when did Emily ever laugh? And Gillian resembled both of them, if anything she took after Emily more than Rose – enough to see what she herself was going to be like one day; what Kate would say she was already turning into.

Kate was talking to a group of women dressed mostly in grey, mauve or navy, and looking neither more nor less depressing than they did at any other time. Yet another sentence for the blog, instantly deleted.

When Kate saw Gillian she broke off, stepped away from the group and took her arm, steering her to a chair.

'God, you look tired. Come on, sit here for a bit. I'll get you some tea—'

'No, it's all right, thanks.' She took the edge of the chair and smiled wearily up at Kate. 'I've had enough tea for one day.'

'Yes, I can imagine. Well, just sit here for a while and I'll keep everyone off. You've spoken to everybody anyway and they'll start trickling away in a minute.'

'Now all the cake's gone,' agreed Gillian. Kate looked sharply at her. 'You've been under too much stress,' she said in her special bright voice, the one she used when the children looked as if they might be going to cry. 'As soon as everything's fixed up here you want to get away for a holiday. You could even go and see your friends in France—'

Gillian got up, muttering 'I forgot something', and hurried away.

The house was hers. Aunt Emily had owned little else, but apart from a legacy to the church and some keepsakes to old friends, she had left everything to Gillian.

... to my niece, Ghislaine Emily Bailie, on condition that she will keep the property intact and continue to reside in the family home ...

'It was my senior colleague who drew up the will,' said the youngish, very correct solicitor. 'I believe he had known your aunt all his life, and I don't think he asked as many questions as he should have. Personally I would have advised against leaving a conditional gift like this. There may well be ways of contesting it or working round it – "reside" is a vague term, for instance, and as her next of kin you should be able to argue that …'

There have always been Starkadders at Cold Comfort, thought Gillian. No doubt Aunt Emily, even if you could have forced her to speak the truth under hypnosis, sincerely believed that it would be best for her niece to live out her life in the same peaceful, safe environment she had known herself. Not even in secret would she have acknowledged any resentment of the unwanted brat who, like her mother before her, had taken away Emily's last faint dreams of escape; any wish to see her niece, too, grow old and withered in the dark house that had devoured her own youth and dragged her into old age long before her time.

You are horrible, Gillian told herself silently, totally horrible – all she wanted was to help you and you're still turning her into a monster. Wasn't it enough that you made her into a monster for your stupid blog, and killed her with it—

'Are you all right?' came the solicitor's voice from far away. 'You look very pale.'

Gillian shook her head to clear it, smiled and got up. 'I'm fine, thanks – I've been a bit tired since, well, you know.'

'Yes, of course. People don't realise how exhausting bereavement is till they experience it. If I were you I'd go away for a break somewhere and worry about all this later.'

Gillian smiled again, thanked her and left, wondering how many other people were going to tell her she looked ill; how many more people would advise her to go away when, clearly, she was going to have to stay.

'Gill, how can you possibly stay on in this house?' Kate brushed last autumn's leaves off a garden chair and sat down while Martha wandered off to try and entice the neighbour's cat, which almost lived in the garden now Aunt Emily wasn't there to chase it out. 'Look how much work it is for a start.'

'I've had a lot to do,' Gillian said defensively, 'I haven't really had a chance to tidy up since the funeral.'

'That's not what I mean. You know the solicitor said there were probably ways of getting round it or even contesting it. What's the point of one person living in a house big enough for six? It was all very well for Emily, she couldn't even imagine being anywhere else and anyway she loved looking after it, didn't she? because it gave her something to do. If you live here it'll just take all your time – or are you thinking of turning it into a B&B or something? Because if you are—'

'Well, I'm not. Apart from anything else, how many tourists ever come here? And as for selling it, who's going to buy a place this size just now? Nobody's buying anything since the crash. But I don't want to try: it's my family home and Aunt Emily would have broken her heart if she'd known I didn't want to stay in it. She never would have left it to me. Even if I could do anything about the will it wouldn't be right.'

There was a long pause; Gillian was well aware that Kate was searching for diplomatic ways to tell her friend not to be stupid. 'Yes, of course,' she produced at last,' you would feel like that, at first anyway. But you can't spend the rest of your life trying to do what she wanted, can you? And it's not as if ... well, it's not like a stately home or something, is it? It's just a house – I mean ...'

'Yes, of course it's just a house,' said Gillian, 'and of course it wouldn't make sense to an incomer.'

Kate looked coldly at her. 'My god, you do sound like your aunt.' A text tone sounded; she whipped her phone out of her bag, tapped briskly and stood up. 'Right, Jack's finished swimming practice so we'll be off. Come on then, Marbs.'

They stood awkwardly for a moment. 'Thanks, Kate,' Gillian said, 'I know you're right really. It's a bit hard to explain.'

'Sure. No worries. Anyway, got to go – I'll be in touch.'

Over the next weeks she saw less of Kate than she had done even when Aunt Emily's illness was at its worst. Kate had started working part-time as a classroom assistant, but that wasn't the main reason. When they did meet they were constrained and wary and talked mostly of the children, Kate's new job and the weather. Gillian knew that she only had to apologise for that remark about incomers and all would be well – bossy Kate might be, but she never bore a grudge – but she couldn't face starting the whole discussion again. It was so much easier just to get up and get through each day, and do what the old ones of Southash expected of her and think of nothing.

One early May morning as she emptied the kitchen bin liner into the dustbin outside the front door, she felt an unfamiliar warmth on her back and looking up, was faintly surprised to see the spring sun, making its presence felt even through the barrier of Aunt Emily's laurels.

Since the funeral she had done little but keep the house and garden in the barest order, after the months of fitting it in around Emily's needs. The sun peering through the gloom of the bushes was no more welcome, for the moment, than a self-righteous neighbour come to remind her of the weeds on the path and the rotted brown leaves still piled in the corners. She turned her back on the busy old fool, went inside and slammed the door.

Yet all the while as she cleaned out cupboards, she was aware of it looking in on her, as if the nosy neighbour had come to remind her of something. At last she gave in and went into the back garden and sat down on the grass, hurriedly leaping up again as the damp soaked through her trousers. 'Shit,' Gillian said, looked round automatically and then remembered that Aunt Emily couldn't hear her.

She moved slowly around the walled space, looking at the few flowers that had survived from last year, wondering vaguely if she should get some seeds and plant anything new. Or should she give up on the garden this year while she got her life in order?

That brought her up short. 'Get your life in order,' she said aloud. 'What the fuck does that mean?' There was, more than likely, a neighbour listening beyond the wall but she didn't care. Old Mrs Blashford would love telling her next visitor that poor Emily Bailie's niece was obviously finding it too much, living all alone in that house. *I heard her talking to herself this morning in the garden – well, I wouldn't like to repeat it but her language! Ah well, she was always peculiar. Didn't she just suddenly drop everything last year and run off to France, leaving poor Emily to fend for herself at her age – I wonder what was behind all that?*

'No,' said Gillian. 'This won't do.' She flopped on to the grass again, ignoring the damp, plucked a blade of grass and sat chewing it and thinking. After a while she got up, and with more energy than she'd felt in many months she ran into the house, grabbed the phone that had hardly been used since the funeral and dialled Kate's landline.

Kate looked up from the screen at last. 'Well,' she said slowly, 'I suppose you had to have something to stop you going mad when you were looking after Emily. All the same, Gill, if people round here knew about it – well, they just wouldn't speak to you. I'm not too happy myself if I'm honest.' Gillian was silently thankful that she had so rarely mentioned Kate in her posts.

'So what are you going to do now?'

'I'm not sure, but I know I've got to try and put things right as far as I can.'

'Does that mean you won't be writing any more of this – this stuff?'

Gillian was astonished. 'Of course I won't! I haven't written a word since, since Aunt Emily died.' She had meant to tell Kate everything, including what had happened when Emily caught her, but at the last moment she was too ashamed. 'You can see that.'

'All right, that's something. As for your friends in France, I don't know. Could you try emailing? They'd probably at least look at it.'

'I've already tried that, and the post,' Gillian said, 'but I've never had an answer.'

'Hmm ... let's think about it. Anyway, I'm glad you told me.'

'So am I,' said Gillian, but walking home later she wondered if that was true. Her confession had been too partial and cowardly to give much relief. Nor had either of them come up with a solution. And for all that she had given up writing for ever, there was a grievance that kept popping up like a thistle in a neatly tended lawn: Kate hadn't even hinted that she thought the blog was any good. In fact she had made it pretty clear that she thought it wasn't.

You still want people to read your rubbish, don't you? she scolded herself. Haven't you done enough damage already?

And then, just as she stepped off the overgrown verge to cross the road to Aunt Emily's house – would she ever be able to think of it as hers? – the solution came to her, in the same way that had started all the upheaval of the last year.

'I'm going back to Les Châtres,' she told the disapproving front door as she let herself in, 'and I'm going to walk straight into the house and just tell them.'

What exactly she would tell them she wasn't yet sure, but there would be time enough to think of that. Now, once again, she had to get out.

17: Ghislaine

Gillian parked the Peugeot in the wide avenue off the main street, switched off the engine and sat back, eyes half closed. Nothing had gone wrong on the journey, but there was so much to arrange and deal with, from cancelling the milk and leaving keys with Kate, through the thrill of her first flight – why ever hadn't she done this before? – to hiring the car and finding her way from the airport. It was only now that she had time to think, and she was as far as ever from knowing what to say or do. What if Amèlie, or Luc, or Beth simply slammed the door on her? Could she just stand there knocking and shouting, in the middle of the afternoon?

Surely she couldn't go there now. It was – yes, she had changed her watch on the plane – half past two. They would be in at their busiest, clearing up after the lunches, or they would if there were any customers, and getting their own meal. And then they, especially Amèlie, would be wanting to snatch some rest before the evening rush.

What rush? This time last year, she had been the only lunchtime visitor and the place was practically empty. She was finding excuses. At least she could go up the road and look. She would leave the Peugot here; somehow it seemed better to walk away, if it came to that, than to roar – or more likely lurch – off in a car, watched by hostile eyes. Besides, if she walked up it would take longer.

She moved slowly, feeling the strangeness of being here again on this road where she had walked almost every day. She had so fiercely crushed all memories of the place, it was almost a shock to find everything still exactly as it had been nearly a year ago. The tall grey houses, the pale light, the beech trees shading the empty midday pavements – it seemed in that moment that she remembered every stone and every leaf. She drew a deep breath of the warm, still air, and it was like a draught of spring water after a dry day.

No longer afraid, she hurried along the last stretch, almost breaking into a run as she caught the first glimpse of the sign on the gate –

The sign on the gate. At first her brain refused to accept it. The old sign must still be there. She was tired and imagining things. She stopped, deliberately closed her eyes, opened them again and there it still was: an estate agent's sale sign. À VENDRE.

Now she had reached the house. The garden was almost wild, much worse than it had been even on that first day, before she and Amèlie had tried to tidy it. She pushed the gate open and went up to the door, but even as she pressed the bell she knew the house was empty. She tried to get a glimpse inside but the shutters were closed.

Back in the street, she couldn't bring herself to walk away but stayed by the gate, staring at the dead windows as if she could force them to open. At last she set off back the way she had come, looking back over her shoulder with every other step, paused again at the corner and then, shaking off her stupor, walked swiftly back past her car and towards the centre. She would ask at the baker's where she used to pick up bread for the family. Mme Beutier always knew everything, and Gillian had had an affection for her ever since the early days of running errands for Amèlie, when her French had struggled with the more complex demands she was making on it. Mme Beutier – large, breathless and inclined to see everyone as a child – had always been kind and patient, coaxing the right words out of her and sometimes urging her to try some little delicacy 'fresh out of the oven, just for you, my dear'.

She remembered Gillian and greeted her with friendliness but some surprise. 'Yes, that's right, the house is for sale. Did you not know that your friends had left? Or are you here on holiday?'

'Actually we, er, lost touch.' Obviously nobody had gossiped. Come to think of it, they wouldn't. 'I had to go back to England, and, well … But I had the chance to come this way for a few days and, um, I forgot to bring the phone number, so …'

She wondered if she sounded as unconvincing and guilty as she felt. Perhaps Mme Beutier put her manner down to rusty French; or perhaps she was too eager to tell her story to notice anything else.

'What a pity, but yes, they closed Les Saules, oh, three months ago it must be now. Poor Amèlie, Mme Martin, she was just not well enough to carry on – the migraines got worse and worse, and the doctor told her she shouldn't have any more stress. And of course those sons of hers aren't much good …' She paused, no doubt remembering she was talking to an outsider, but Gillian nodded understandingly and she carried on, 'in fact I heard the younger one, the one with the little boy – what was his name, we hardly ever saw him in here – Luc, of course – I believe he and his wife separated. She was English like you, wasn't she?'

'Yes, that's right. Separated! How sad. Do you know where they all are now?'

'No, I think the girl, the wife, what was her name?'

'Beth.'

'Bet, yes, I think she was going back to England. And Amèlie's gone to stay with her sister in Orléans, but I don't know about Luc. Amèlie hated having to give up, but it was too much for her, anyone could see that.'

Gillian nodded again, remembering how exhausted Amèlie had looked after a day's work and how often her face was set in pain. A silence fell, and Mme Beutier made as if to get back to work. Hoping she wasn't blushing, Gillian asked, 'And Hervé? The other brother? Do you know …'

Mme Beutier wasn't interested in Hervé. 'I don't really know him. Yes, now you mention it I think he works in Orléans, but I haven't seen him in here for, oh, years. I haven't lived here all my life, you know. Nor has Amèlie, of course – it was her husband's family that had the house. I remember *him*, but he was very ill even then. I have heard he was a bit of a tyrant, not that you'd ever hear Amèlie complain about anything—'

Gillian started to edge to the door. She needed to be by herself, to sit down and think. 'Well, thank you so much, Madame, it was so nice to see you again. Actually I think I'll just have one of your lovely tartes au fraises to take with me ...'

She went to the little public garden off the square, sat on a bench in the shade and ate her pastry. She was still bewildered, but the overwhelming sensation was of relief. From the moment she had seen the empty house the dread had lurked in her mind that Amèlie might have died – even worse, that it might in some obscure way have been Gillian's fault. Only now, licking sweet strawberry-flavoured crumbs off her fingers in the sunshine, did she see how absurd and egotistical her thoughts had been. 'You must think you're some writer,' she said to herself, laughing silently at the image of rows of people reading her articles and falling down dead. Like the World's Funniest Joke in the old Monty Python sketch.

So Amèlie had finally given up the battle to keep up the family tradition that had never been hers in the first place. Was she happy now, with her sister? Gillian wondered what she would do with herself without any responsibilities. She had never seemed to have any interests of her own. And how she would miss Hugo if Beth really had taken him back to England.

She brushed off the last of the crumbs and stood up, looking around the empty park. Just on the other side of the low wall she could see the edge of the square. Today was – what? Thursday, which meant tomorrow was market day. In the early morning all this peace would be gone; there would be the clatter of stalls being set up, cars backing and unloading, arguments and jokes. There would be bright fabrics spread out, and cheeses, and chickens slowly roasting in their basting juices. People would come crowding in, tasting and touching, grumbling at prices but happy, surely, because it was market day in early summer and the Loire was bright under the sky …

She slumped back onto the bench. All the energy that had carried her here was gone; she could not move for misery. How could she ever explain to anyone what she had lost? How ridiculous it sounded: 'I lived and worked here one summer. I was very happy here, but when I came back the family I knew had moved away.' Because that was all she was ever going to be able to tell anyone.

Anyway. She stood up again. She wasn't going to give up just like that: her flight wasn't till tomorrow, and this afternoon she would go back to the house and get the estate agent's phone number. They might be able to help her contact Amèlie – or didn't they do things like that? She had never dealt with an estate agent in her life. Well, never mind; if she posed as a prospective buyer she would find out more than Mme Beutier had been able to tell her.

It darted into her mind that the price of a large French family home, in poor repair, might be comparable to that of a well-maintained family house in a southern English village; but the thought was unreal and soon floated away.

As she left the park another and more concrete thought struck her: she had nowhere to stay tonight. She must have been thinking the Trafic was still in the meadow behind the house waiting to welcome her home. The afternoon was passing; should she find somewhere right away? No, she'd go back to Les Saules first, collect the car and find a hotel afterwards.

She set off up the same road she had walked yesterday, but without yesterday's nervous excitement it seemed much longer. She reached the corner of the road as before, and there immediately was the For Sale sign – how could she not have seen it straight away? She reached into her bag and scrawled the agent's number on a crumpled receipt, wondering whether to call it straight away or go and look for the company's office in town. Maybe the latter would be best.

She pushed the paper into the bag and zipped it shut. That was that then. She jerked the bag up on to her shoulder and, already half turning back towards the town, stopped for a last look at the house. The door into the bar was open.

For a moment she just stood looking at it: was her mind playing tricks again? Then she pushed through the gate and up the path as she had done yesterday, and reached the door before doubts took hold of her again and she stopped. What was she going to say? She lifted a hand to knock and paused again. She remembered Amèlie putting the phone down on her, Beth's disgust, all that had happened.

Well, there was nothing to lose. She knocked, but her shrinking knuckles made hardly any sound on the heavy old wood. She tried again and then, hearing no sound inside, very cautiously pushed the door a little further until she could peer inside. The bar was dark after the brightness of the afternoon, but she could see a figure inside, near the door that led back into the house. Stooping over the little table by the door, back turned to her, but she knew at once who it was. She tried to say 'Hervé?' but no sound came. She tried again, and this time he heard her and turned. He stood perfectly still, staring at her. With no idea what to say she took one step forward, and then another; then she reached him and he caught her and held her, tighter than she had ever been held, ever, and in that moment all fear and loneliness seemed to fall away.

After a long while they drew apart; he started to speak and then stopped, looking closely into her face.

'What is it?'

'You look ... Ghislaine, what's been happening to you?'

She laughed – him too? 'You mean I look dreadful, don't you?' She went on over his sound of protest, 'Well, I know I do. It's been ... things have been difficult. My aunt died in the winter.'

They sat in Amèlie's huge kitchen, now dusty and almost empty, and she told him, in fits and jerks and with many false starts, about the long grey months with Aunt Emily. There came a point when she couldn't speak any more and slumped in her seat, staring down at the table. Hervé put an arm round her and said, 'You must have loved your aunt very much – more than I realised.'

She lifted her head and looked at him in surprise. His face was full of concern; it would be so easy just to nod, and let her eyes fill with pretty tears, and be held and comforted in the way she had been starved for all her life.

Instead she got up and went to the window, and looked out over the garden. Still turned away from him she said, 'No, I didn't. I never loved her any more than she did me. By the time she died I hated the sight of her.'

Hervé came and stood beside her, not touching her but looking intently at her profile. 'And yet you stayed with her and looked after her.'

Again she longed to agree, if only by silence; to seem to be the person he thought she was. To seem to be someone who deserved love.

But what was the use? She said, 'It's my fault she's dead.'

He only said, 'Tell me what happened.' So she told him about the blog, and the relief it had brought her night after night to savage the helpless old woman and their neighbours; and how she had loved the responses she got, and to please her invisible audience grown ever more vitriolic. And not looking at him, speaking almost in a whisper, she told him how Aunt Emily had seen it and what the shock had done to her; so that the last clear thought she had in her life was that the niece she had so unwillingly taken in and cared for had secretly hated her, had taken pleasure in betraying and humiliating her. She told him how Emily had wheezed for air, clutching at nothing; how her eyes had rolled and gone bloodshot.

When she finished Hervé was silent for a while. That's it, she thought, I may as well leave now. Did I ever really think everything was just going to work out? At last he said, 'Did you know that I killed my father?'

She jerked round to face him. 'That you – what did you say?'

'Well, it's what Luc would tell you if he was being honest – it's certainly what he thinks, and if my mother wasn't so discreet – and so loyal – she might even say the same.' He laughed at her astounded face. 'Let's go out and find something to eat. And afterwards I'll tell you what happened, but there are too many things I want to ask you first.' He locked the outer door and stuffed the key in his pocket. 'In the first place, what brings you here just now?'

She tried to think how to begin as they crossed the front garden, now so wild the grass brushed her ankles, and turned down the avenue towards the town and the river. 'It was mostly that I wanted to see your mother. I wanted to tell her how sorry I am about the article. I don't know what made me write all that.' She tried to recapture the way she'd felt that day: sullen and vengeful, like a child excluded from a game.

'Well,' said Hervé, 'I probably shouldn't have, but I enjoyed it. Especially the part about Luc.'

'You read it?'

Yes. Beth almost threw it at me – she really acted as if I was responsible for it in some way – so of course I read it.

And yes, I can see how my family might have seemed that way to you.'

'No, they didn't, not really. It was me. I don't know what I was thinking. Amèlie's been so good to me, and I really hurt her, didn't I?'

'She's never mentioned what happened to me, but yes, she would be hurt. All the same, she will understand if you explain to her.'

'I hope so. Of course she was much too angry to speak to me at the time, and no wonder.'

This time it was Hervé who looked at her in surprise. 'You tried to reach her then?'

'Of course – she hung up on me, and I had no idea what was wrong until Beth told me. I emailed too, and wrote by post. Didn't either of them mention it?'

'No!' said Hervé, so loudly that a woman passing on the inside of the pavement turned to look at them. He went on, quietly, 'If I'd known – Ghislaine, I would have tried to find you, tried to contact the magazine, done something, but I was so sure there was no point. I thought Beth must be right about why you were here.'

'Did she tell you I was only staying in France to look for material for my writing?'

'Yes, and why not? It made perfect sense. It always seemed strange that a woman like you should be living like that, in an old camping-car – and, well ...' He hesitated.

'What, Hervé?'

'I thought I must have imagined that you were, that you seemed, I don't know – interested in me.'

'A woman like me.' She laughed with both pleasure and embarrassment, thinking, Hervé, nobody but you has ever...

In the side-street brasserie where Gillian used to go for coffee they found a tiny table pushed under the window. The owner recognised her at once, but looked vaguely at

Hervé. 'You know the town much better than I do now, don't you?' he said. 'I never did come back much after I left. I'm only here now to make sure there's nothing important left behind – most of the furniture's being sold along with the house, now my mother's gone to live in Orléans and – but you don't even know that, do you?'

'Yes I do, and about Luc and Beth separating. Mme Beutier told me.'

'Who?'

'Mme Beutier – you know, the baker in Rue Foulques-Nerra.'

'No, I don't think so – like I said, you do know the town better than I do. It sounds as if your friend Mme Beutier knows all the family except me, anyway.'

'She didn't seem to know much about you, no.'

Hervé gave her that sudden, sweet smile again. 'You asked her about me?'

'Yes, of course, I ... I did try to find you before – online, I mean. But—' She stopped, seeing a waiter approaching, and when he had gone said, 'Anyway, about Luc and Beth. When did it happen?'

'From what my mother said, one day last winter Beth just announced that she'd had enough. Things had got worse – Maman's health certainly had, and there were so many days when she couldn't carry on at all. And Luc – you can probably imagine what Luc was like.'

'Hervé, if I'd stayed on, do you think Amèlie could have kept the place going?'

'A little while longer, maybe. But Luc and Beth were always going to separate sometime – you could see that, couldn't you? And how long would Maman and Luc have just kept going as they were? You didn't cause this, Ghislaine. Not that it would have been any tragedy if you had. But you didn't.' He smiled across at her. 'You can't go feeling helpless all your life and still think everything that happens is your fault.'

It was so exactly what she had been thinking that she laughed too, more in surprise than anything else. 'How did you know that's how I've always felt?'

'Oh, I'm no better. We're quite alike, it seems to me. I've wasted a lot of time thinking that way.'

'When my father was alive,' Hervé said as they wandered through the outskirts, 'the only thing he cared about was keeping that house.' He looked back along the darkening streets. 'That house: it had fields once, it had its own land. I forget now how long his family had farmed it, though I was told often enough. They had cattle, they grew grapes and so on. My grandfather was either unlucky or stupid – which version we got depended on my father's mood – but either way there wasn't much left for us to inherit.

'Even when Luc and I were boys my parents were still trying to work the land that was left. But however hard they worked it was too little, hardly enough to keep us going, and the town was growing up around us. At last my father gave in and sold most of the land for building; in the end there was just that little meadow where you kept your camping-car, and the garden. Of course the house was still much too big and too expensive, and my father didn't have good health even then. They should have sold the house. It was just the time city people were starting to buy houses in the countryside, all over France.'

'And the rosbifs,' Gillian remarked.

He smiled. 'Yes, well, obviously Papa wasn't going to risk a rosbif getting his hands on our ancestral home. In fact anyone from beyond Orléans was a foreigner to him, and anyway the one thing he cared about was making sure that we Martins stayed in the house we'd always lived in. And so that's how the idea of Les Saules was born.'

They turned along the river path as a heron flapped towards the willows. 'And when we came home from school Luc and I helped with the few guests we got, or ran errands or worked on that miserable plot of land.

Vegetables for the kitchen now, rather than potatoes for the market, but either way we never seemed to be getting much out of it.'

'I can't imagine you doing all that,' she said and then was angry with herself. Wasn't that just telling him he was useless, as she had so often been told herself?

But he only laughed slightly and said, 'Well, I was even less use than you might imagine. And I hated it – even more than I'd hated the farming work. At least that was work that had a point to it; but to a boy that age, running around after a lot of lazy holidaymakers ... and besides, I always knew I wanted to study history. It was fairly annoying for my father, obviously – I was quite happy finding out everything about the history of our house, but when it came to cleaning the windows or fixing a tile I was always somewhere else.'

'And Luc?'

'Luc didn't – doesn't – mind the work itself, but in those days he always wanted his own place. He wanted to be a chef once, go away to Paris and get some serious training. And he fought our father more and more as he got older. My mother was afraid of Papa' – his voice faltered for a moment – 'and so was I, even after I grew up I suppose. But for all Luc would shout at him, and they even came to blows once, in the end it was Luc who was prepared to give up his plans and work for the family business. I was the one who let them all down.'

Gillian remembered that evening when Hervé had sat letting Luc jeer at him, making no attempt to defend himself. 'Is that what you think?'

'Yes, I suppose I still do – at least I can see why Luc feels so bitter. And it's true as far as ... well, if I'd given up everything like Luc it's possible that we might have managed. My father had a heart attack, you see. And the doctor told him very clearly that if he carried on working the way he was, it would kill him. I'd started my degree by then, and my parents wanted me to leave the university and come and work in Les Saules. So one evening he told me there was to be no arguing: that was what I was going to do.'

He stared out over the water; it was almost too dark to see his face, but she could hear the way his voice slowed, as if each word hurt like a pebble in the throat.

'My father was shouting, furious, growing darker and darker in the face – my mother was terrified that he would have another attack and kept begging me to give in. But this I could not do. Finally he came at me with his fists raised and I …' He swallowed.

'Defended yourself?'

He sighed. 'That's how it seemed to me. But I was a grown man, a young one, and he was growing old. I only meant to push him off, but he kept on hitting, so I ... and then he fell and he was hurt. My mother rushed over to him; I went to help, but she only looked up at me and said, "Just leave the house." Her voice I will never forget. I left straight away – I don't even remember where I went that night. When I managed to speak to my mother again, Papa had already been taken to hospital with another heart attack. Within a week he was dead.'

Gillian pressed her cheek against his shoulder and slid her hand round his arm. He put his hand over hers and said, 'It's very good to be with you, Ghislaine.'

They were silent for a while, still looking along the river. Presently she said, 'What does your mother think now?'

'I don't think she blames me for his death, not exactly, though I know she'll never be able to forget what happened. After the autopsy the doctor told her his heart was badly diseased, so … Of course she never told anyone what happened. But she realised it would have happened sooner or later anyway – as it would with your aunt, you see. You can't kill a healthy person with a shock.'

'No, of course. But your mother ... it must have been a terrible thing for her, losing him like that.'

'Yes ... even though he really didn't treat her very well, in the later years anyway. But she was very young when they married and he was a lot older. Everything had to be the way he wanted it. By the time he died, she'd given her whole life to it; making the farm work, then keeping the house going. That's why she worked so hard to manage the *pension* after he died, I suppose. How could she admit that it had all been for nothing?'

'But in the end she had to.'

'In the end she had to, and it was probably the best thing she's ever done. I see her more often now she's in Orléans and I never remember her as happy as this. She has time now – she has friends, she reads a lot – and she's even taking English lessons, can you imagine that?'

'English lessons? Whatever for?'

'So she can go to England and visit Hugo.'

'Oh, yes, I see. I don't suppose Beth would bring him here.'

'I doubt it; I believe he'll be spending holidays with Luc when he's a bit older, but I don't think they've worked it all out yet. Luc did find a job in Le Mans, but that's about all I know. Maman misses the boy, and so do I.'

She remembered him swinging Hugo into the air by the mirabelle tree. 'Yes, of course you do.' They started slowly back to the town. The river was black now, lit only by the half moon and the dim lamps.

Just before they reached the house he said, 'But you will go on writing now, won't you?'

She felt a faint squirm of guilt; even now, there was still that part of her, shut away but never quite silenced, that was constantly trying to weave stories out of whatever came to hand. 'How can I after all that's happened? All I ever seem to do is cause trouble when I write anything.'

'Do you? What about all the people who wrote to tell you how much you were helping them?' She'd forgotten all about the people who commented on her pages; hadn't given them a thought since Emily died. Was it possible that some of those people might want to hear from her again, even now? Or that others might?

'That's true,' she said slowly. 'All the same ... it's as if I'm a different person when I write, and not even – I mean, I don't even *like* this person and, well, I don't think you would either. I can't seem to help it.'

'I'll take the risk,' said Hervé. 'You have to go on writing; you know it, don't you, Ghislaine? That's who you are.'

She stood still for a moment. All those half-formed stories, all those words and images that wouldn't go away – could she really let them in again? Could that possibly be in her future – listening to the voice inside and learning to let it speak?

In the most silent of the small hours, she half woke. There was a moment of confusion; was she in her heavy single bed in Southash? on the lumpy mattress in the old Trafic? Her mind slowly cleared; she was in the large double room in Les Saules, the one with the view of the garden, and Hervé was asleep beside her with one arm lying heavy across her body. Would there come a time when things like this would be ordinary, part of everyday life? Just now it seemed like a miracle: that she, that they should be here, in this perfect stillness. She shifted a little closer, sliding back into a half-sleep.

She saw her life winding along like the river, creeping onward from its beginnings in the dark house, under the dank, ivy-choked banks of her slow, slow childhood. Then came the drab, dammed years of study and work, work and home – stagnant almost, never getting faster or slower. Now and then the current would swirl round a stone, stirring its monotony for a moment – a good day, a bad day, nothing stood out at this distance.

Then the dam breaking and the rush outward into new landscapes of shifting currents and radiant light. The flow into the wide sweep of the Loire, the willows, the sand islands and the herons. It was here that every shimmer, every lap of water against the river bank was a touch, a quiver of life. Here only to breathe in the air, to linger under the willows in the evening was to be nourished and grow strong. And then the river twisted and snaked back on itself and she was hurled, feebly slapping against the current with hands like tiny, useless oars, back into the dark; and there all movement had stopped, all breath.

And now she had fought her way to the grey-green willows and the sands again. Whether she would stay here or go onward she did not yet know, but she would never go back.

An unfamiliar sound disturbed her, and then she was jolted into full consciousness by a thought that made her sit upright and say aloud: 'My flight leaves at eleven!'

Now she saw what had woken her: Hervé, already dressed, was at the window pulling back one of the shutters. *'Comment? Mais ...'* He abruptly let it go, causing it to swing back against the wall, and a second later was sitting on the side of the bed, holding her by the shoulders. 'You ... you're leaving? Ghislaine ...' She realised that till this moment she had given not one thought to today; as if everything had been resolved already.

But then it had really, hadn't it? She started to say something, something practical about catching the flight and going back just to arrange things, but it was too absurd, too ridiculous even to think of going back to the dark house now, alone, with the sun climbing up through the lime trees and Hervé afraid, actually afraid that she might not want to stay here! So instead she laughed and shook her head, and he let out a long breath and laughed too, into her tangled hair.

Voices came faintly from the avenue beyond the garden; a car door slammed and an engine started. Hervé stood up. 'I'm going out to see what I can find for breakfast – all we've got here is coffee.'

'Croissants from Mme Beutier,' said Gillian at once.

'In the Rue Foulques-Nerra – where else? Mme Beutier's it is – I'll be back in no time.' He leaned over to kiss her and a moment later she heard him running down the stairs.

Gillian got up and dressed, peering into the dusty mirror on the wardrobe door. The light here was still dim; she went to the window and opened the shutters as wide as they would go.

There would be so many things to arrange today: calling the airport to start with, and where should she take the hired car? Which, now she thought of it, was still parked well out of sight of the house, with her travelling bag inside it, not to mention all her papers. She would have to call Kate too, and what was she going to say? Then there would be more, much more: just little matters such as what, exactly, she was going to do about her house, finding work, the rest of her life. But even as part of her mind was listing tasks, forming and discarding plans, wondering what would happen, the memory of yesterday, the thought of today, brought a warm rush of happiness that swept everything out of its way.

She turned back to the mirror; she could see clearly now. She laughed at the state of her hair, and was trying to tidy it with her fingers when, with no warning, the voice was back: *Well, you're looking very pleased with yourself for someone who seems to be making herself homeless and penniless, aren't you, dear? So what exactly are your plans now?* 'I don't have any plans,' she told the mirror, 'but I know I'm not going back.' *I see. And could you tell me exactly what the attraction is? A man you hardly know? A crumbling old house? Or a country where you have no job and no roots, and that you really know very little about?*

'All of them!' she answered aloud, and now at last she recognised the voice that had echoed through all her years; the voice that had wrapped itself round all her most secret thoughts like a clammy hand round her neck. It wasn't poor Aunt Emily's at all, though it might have started that way. It was hers: the voice of her own self-hatred, her own terror of life, and now it was gone. Gillian was gone.

Outside she heard hurrying footsteps and turned back to the window to see Hervé coming up the path to the front door. Ghislaine took a last look out over the garden and the wakening streets, and beyond to the glint of the river, and went down into the morning.

THE END

Printed in Great Britain
by Amazon